CW00525328

THE LEASH

ALSO BY FRANÇOISE SAGAN

Bonjour Tristesse
A Certain Smile
Those Without Shadows
Aimez-Vous Brahms?
The Wonderful Clouds
La Chamade
The Heartkeeper
A Few Hours of Sunlight
Scars on the Soul
Lost Profile
Silken Eyes
The Unmade Bed
The Painted Lady
The Still Storm
Incidental Music
Le Chien Couchant
With Fondest Regards
Engagements of the Heart
Painting in Blood

THE LEASH

by

Françoise Sagan

Translated from the French
by
Christine Donougher

First published in Great Britain in 1991 by
Allison & Busby
An imprint of Virgin Publishing
338 Ladbroke Grove
London W10 5AH

Originally published in France by Julliard
under the title *La laisse*

Printed and bound in Great Britain by
Mackays of Chatham PLC, Chatham, Kent

ISBN 0 85031 867 X

FOR NICOLE WISNIAK GRUMBACH

Chapter One

I stole back into the darkness of our bedroom. It was a very feminine room, with Indian draperies, in which Laurence's perfume, exquisite and heavy, as ever hung upon the air, and, as ever, would probably leave me with a migraine, especially since my wife's mother had persuaded her, after two or three positive reactions to skin tests during her adolescence, to sleep with the shutters and windows closed.

But I had just spent five minutes in my bathroom with all the windows open, breathing in the bracing fresh air, the country air of Paris at dawn, and I was feeling really good as I bent over Laurence, my sleeping beauty. Her long black hair clung to the classic bone structure of her face, giving her that look of a Romanesque virgin that I had noticed in her from the very first. She sighed. I bent lower, and placed my lips on her neck. Despite her obsession with slimness, she was very pleasing, in full bloom like this, with her pink complexion and black eyelashes. I drew back the sheet to uncover her a little more, but she pulled it up again over her shoulders as though shocked.

"Oh please! No! Such nonsense . . . not at this hour in the morning! Really! Behave yourself!"

Like many women, when you thought of making love before she did, she was perverse enough to express disgust: "Oh, that's all you ever think about!" Or: "Don't you love me any more?" in a disembodied voice, when it was the other way round. Passionate in love-making – to cite the classic occasions – Laurence nonetheless spoke of love as prostitutes do not, only society women: in a coarse, puerile way. But then, what woman does talk properly of love? To my knowledge, men do no better.

"Of course," I said, "you're annoyed."

"I'm not annoyed, I'm upset."

"Upset? What for? What have I done?" I asked, already resigned to being in the wrong.

And sure enough, it seemed that at a dinner the previous evening I had exchanged some "suggestive" remarks with the young wife of a banker – whereas I recalled having had difficulty in making any sense at all of our conversation.

More significantly, it transpired that this banker-husband was a close friend of my father-in-law (an odious character with whom we had fallen out seven years before, ever since he had declared that I was nothing but an utter layabout, and that I was getting married with the sole object of stealing his only child, his innocent, and extremely rich, little girl). Since veiled defiance was not his style but rather noisy accusation, Laurence had been deeply upset by this. To have someone go and tell him now that, not content with stealing his daughter, I was also making a fool of her, greatly vexed Laurence, who after seven years was still distressed by her father's opprobrium and estrangement.

She and I had met two or three years after I finished studying piano at the Conservatoire, and we were married almost at once, despite the doubts her father entertained about my career as a virtuoso. And he would have been entitled, seven years later, to entertain even greater doubts (or fewer) had I not by chance been asked to write the music for a film. The film in question had been a real success and my music a genuine triumph: the music had since been performed by all the singers, orchestras and musicians of Europe, and now of the USA. So I was going to be receiving some money and be in a position to return to Laurence a little of what I owed her. Yet, oddly, Laurence, who had taken my years of idleness and failure very well, proved to be alarmed by this magnificent stroke of luck, and was even so disturbed by it that I was cross with her for not sharing my satisfaction and good fortune.

The success of this melody had been so remarkable, that people had actually tried to seek out its composer. Appalled by this, Laurence had at once whisked me away to the Baltic to escape the "vulgar media", as she scornfully put it. In my absence, they had fallen back on the film director and cast, and we had returned to a Paris totally indifferent to my good self. Nevertheless, Laurence's fury and annoyance – and her wariness – remained unabated, as though I were responsible.

Then again, much as I blamed her for the displeasure my success caused her, I could not help understanding it. Laurence had married – or wanted to marry – a famous pianist, a virtuoso, which I had not become (but which she had never blamed me for not becoming). On the other hand, she had not married a composer of light music; it was not for someone who wrote "smash hits" that she had left her family, defied her father and his threats to disinherit her, and for seven years forced upon her snobbish, music-loving friends, as her husband and as a musician, a man they described as her gigolo – with some unfairness, it must be added, since Laurence was my age, a great beauty and a passionate music-lover.

She had in any event announced, on marrying me, that art was more important than money: to members of her family, a ludicrous assertion (but the truth of which I hoped I had been able to demonstrate to her, in ways that followed from it – and ways that were, according to her, pleasurable). She'd had to fight to get me accepted into this social circle that, like any other, was snobbish, treacherous and amoral; and once I had their approval, it was natural that my father-in-law should despise me. The poor fellow had already had to come to terms with the fact that his own wife had left us her entire fortune when she died – for Laurence's mother was the only pleasant person in that family, indeed, she was positively likeable, and I have to say that, had it not been so providential, her death would have greatly saddened me. Anyway, to return to the present, I could see very well that I would have to comfort Laurence.

"My darling, I'm not unfaithful to you and you know it! Yes, yes," I insisted, "you know it! By choice, *my* choice. The fact that you pay for my food, accommodation, clothes, pocket money, cigarettes, car, insurance . . ."

"Stop it!" she cried.

Laurence could not bear the itemizing of her largesse towards me, or rather she could not bear me to be the one to itemize it. Quite the contrary, she saw in this a disturbing masochism, as if recalling her generosity and the miseries she was sparing me gave me no additional reason to love her.

"Stop it!" she cried, leaning forward. "Stop it!" she cried, throwing her hands round my neck. "Stop it!" she said, placing her cheek against mine.

"There, there," I said, cradling her in my arms. "Really now, you saw that poor woman, all skin and bones, with hair like straw, and her nose in the air? Didn't you?"

"Maybe. Well, yes . . ."

"You're not going to tell me that's the sort of beauty I go for?" I asked her, laughing myself at this insanity. "Take a look at yourself, if you please."

And she nodded her head, murmured "Yes, of course" (as though her own face had no charm – but women possess only the logic of their own happiness). Meanwhile, I would steer well clear of the lady in question next time.

I stood up.

"Good! Well, I'm going to extort some money from Not-a-sou!" I abruptly declared, laughing as hard as I could at a well-worn joke, but one that I hoped Laurence would laugh at too, giving me time to get across the room and out of the door before the expression on her face turned from amusement to reproach, as mine turned from amusement to guilt. For even though Laurence did not say so, she could never bear my absences – whether this was a matter of nerves or emotion, I do not know. But her reaction seemed remarkable after seven years of marriage, and one that ought to be registered on the marriage's plus side.

I had time to get through the door and to start down the stairs, on my way to Not-a-sou. The Not-a-sou I had just mentioned was the producer at my record company – the one which had recorded my song "Showers"; it was called Delta Blues Productions. Despite all his Americanisms and incessant trips to New York, the name Palassous betrayed his Latin origins just as much as his tightly fitting suits and two-tone shoes. Ferdinand Palassous had an appalling reputation as an unscrupulous, greedy producer, but one also capable of rewarding his protégés if they earned him some money, which I had; and if they demanded it from him forcefully enough, which I was about to, with the help of my best friend, Coriolan Latelot.

Coriolan was my age and shared my past. We were born in the same year in the same street of the same arrondissement. We had been pupils at the same lycée, done our military service in the same barracks, shared the same girls and the same shortage of funds until Laurence's arrival on the scene. They could not stand each other, their mutual antipathy dating from day one, an antipathy I would have been able to live with had they not insisted on taking every opportunity to make it obvious to each other, she criticizing him for not being a layabout but acting like one, and he criticizing her for being bourgeois and, what's more, overplaying her hand: teasing that had in time turned to grievance.

Coriolan and I had agreed to meet outside the Lion de Belfort, our usual café headquarters. Coriolan worked at the end of rue Daguerre, in his garage workshop, and the office from which he operated as a bookmaker was at the far end of rue Froidevaux, only two minutes from our apartment.

Of all the property owned by her mother, Laurence and I had chosen this fifth-floor apartment in a building at the top of the hill, on boulevard Raspail, just beyond boulevard Montparnasse. This put me three hundred metres not only from Coriolan but also from the neighbourhood where I had grown up – information I had carefully concealed from Laurence. Had she ever found out, I knew she would have certainly chosen from among the range of her family's properties an apartment further away from this neighbourhood which I knew inside-out. Laurence would have liked to change my circumstances entirely, and to give me – as well as a new life, new love and new comfort – a new arrondissement. The abduction of her musician was not so total as she would have wished, but the few bids to move house that she had made subsequently had met with a lack-lustre response. Of course, of course, not for anything in the world would I have tried to oppose her decisions or thwart a happiness that was, after all, mine too; of course everything inside me held me back from standing up to her. But at the same time any conflict had always cost me almost womanish migraines, heavy silences, endless nervous exhaustion, which had discouraged her, as well, from crossing me too often. In short, there we had let the matter rest – that is to say, in boulevard Raspail.

So I went off to see Coriolan, and although our meeting place was only a short distance away, I took my car, a superb coupé which Laurence had given me for my birthday three years ago. It was a beautiful black beast, precise, powerful, as lithe as a piece of music by Ravel, and gleaming, too, that morning in a spell of sunshine. I took a detour down boulevard Raspail and boulevard Montparnasse, then along avenue de l'Observatoire, so as to enjoy my car and the purring sound it made. For Paris was empty. The pedestrians had tired of putting on and taking off their raincoats to keep up with the bright intervals and showers, and taken shelter once and for all; and the wet, deserted streets lay smooth and shining like huge sea-lions, beneath the bonnet of my car. The light quivered and I had the impression of gliding along, effortlessly and noiselessly, inside one of those bubbles – half sunshine, half rain; half air, half liquid; half cloud, half wind – one of those rapturous moments that defy scientific description, which fluctuating weather conditions sometimes happen to grant us. On the other hand, the gale of the night before had spared no thought for the fate of those leaves that, whatever their age, it had furiously separated from the trees; from darkest russet leaves to freshest green shoots of artless simplicity, from scalloped edge to the white line of their central spine. And when I automatically turned on my wipers, I saw them sweep bundles of these leaves across the windscreen surface, mingling them with the sinuous trickles of rain. Whilst these zealous instruments divided the leaves into two droves before casting them down into the scuttle-panel, their last pasturing-ground, I saw those leaves flatten themselves on the cold glass and beg me, face to face, to do for them I know not what – something my cold city-dweller's eyes did not understand.

This fit of sentimentality (in a fellow as well balanced as I was generally thought to be) should come as no surprise. In certain domains, mankind knows nothing; and it occasionally depressed me to imagine, to suppose the existence of nerves, pain, cries, screams in all that we can touch, in all that we can spoil, in all that I personally felt to be vulnerable and silent – horribly silent. As a musician, I knew that our dogs are more receptive than we are, that the human ear does not catch one-hundredth of the sounds emitted around it. I knew too that crushed grass makes a noise that cannot be imitated by the most sophisticated of synthesizers.

"At last!"

The door opened and Coriolan's face appeared in the doorway. Although at that moment full of mirth, it was the face of an embittered Spaniard. Certain disparities between character and appearance can be unnerving, but it was downright scary in Coriolan's case. This man was the very incarnation of a disgraced Spanish nobleman, so much so that his best friends preferred him sad, though they loved him dearly. As for women, very few could bear to wake up in bed with a cheery chappie, having succumbed to a nobleman. This often obliged Coriolan, during evenings when he would rather have been fun, to keep up an appearance of mournfulness; without which, he would also have failed to win the favours of his female companion.

When he was serious, he was impressive and delightful, as a Spanish nobleman might be charming and seductive; when he laughed, he caused as much embarrassment and offence as a conman pretending to be a Spanish nobleman. The unfairness of his fate would have defeated more than most. But not him, for he had the self-respect, courage and pride that his face promised, even though his near-penury led people to label these virtues as unawareness, stubbornness and arrogance. In any event he was my friend, my best friend, and now, since my marriage, my only friend – Laurence not having the same tastes as mine in friendship.

"Where are we going?" he asked, settling his long legs in the front seat, and looking pleased as he always did whenever he saw me. I felt a rush of gratitude towards him. He was the most loyal, the most thoughtful man anyone could hope for. I glanced at him: his clothes told of his financially disastrous state, but he would not accept a sou that came from Laurence. And for the past seven years, that was all I had.

"It's absolutely imperative that I get some money out of Not-a-sou," I said with all the more conviction. " 'Showers' is playing everywhere, but he claims that SACEM* hasn't paid him."

"That's daylight robbery!" said Coriolan calmly. "That's all you ever hear! Every time you earn . . . say, ten francs, that creep pockets one and a half – just because the account is sent to him and he does the arithmetic, can you believe it? And now he doesn't even pay up . . . that's the limit! What's he like?"

"Oh!" I replied, "oh, he's from Nice, or Toulon, I'm not sure. He's all right, but he tries to pass himself off as an honest-to-God New Yorker. You'll see."

"I'll take care of him," Coriolan declared, rubbing his hands.

Then, at the top of his voice, he began to hum a Schubert quartet that had not let him be, as he put it, for a month. For

*Société des Auteurs, Compositeurs et Editeurs de Musique.

this garage mechanic-cum-bookmaker was an expert on music, one of the most highly respected by the major European magazines, and he was constantly being consulted by the world's greatest musicians, so astounding were his memory, his musical knowledge and his insights into every kind of music. But he refused to make a profession of them, on account of some unknown romanticism or yearning.

Having broken off his quartet, Coriolan turned to me:

"What about your wife? Is she getting used to your success?"

Someone or other had told him of our differences. A bit irritated, I replied rather drily:

"Yes and no . . . You know how she would prefer me to be a great pianist . . ."

Coriolan burst out laughing.

"Come, come now! She can't really believe in that for a second. Not even her! You haven't been working for a good three years now . . . What do you do in your famous studio? You read detective stories, don't you? You wouldn't be able to play any Czerny now . . . She can't be that stupid! You, a virtuoso, now? You have to practise for that, my friend, as you well know!"

"So what is it, do you think, that she wants of me? And what did she want of me to start with?"

"What did she want of you? What does she want of you? Nothing, my friend, nothing. Well, yes: everything! She wants you to be there and do nothing. Haven't you got the message yet? She wants *you*, full stop! She's no Romanesque virgin, she's a vampire."

At that point the telephone rang and Coriolan, subdued, fell silent: this, to him, was the most fascinating thing about the car. I picked up the receiver and of course heard nothing: there was no one at the other end. Only Laurence knew my number and she would never have disturbed me for no reason. Yet another mistake at the exchange. But here we were, outside my producer's building.

Palassous's premises were a caricature of the Champs-Elysées office. After a rather shabby-looking staircase, there was a door on the second floor that was somewhat dirty but nevertheless bore a black marble plate with "Delta Blues" in silver lettering.

"Why Delta Blues?" sneered Coriolan. "Why not Depression Niçoise?" he even suggested, following me over the excessively thick-pile hallway carpet. A secretary-starlet informed us that the producer was talking on the phone to some other big shot, and indeed he was in deep discussion. But he felt obliged upon seeing us to adopt a hurried tone of voice and a pained expression, yet for all that without interrupting his conversation; nor did he feel obliged to apologize when he came off the phone. I'd grown used to businessmen being rude: Laurence's friends all had jobs or positions that allowed them to look down on my enforced idleness – even if they secretly envied me – and to make their contempt obvious. However, coming from someone like Palassous, for whom I had been providing a handsome living – so I was told – for some time now, I felt this attitude was taking things a little too far.

"And how is your charming wife?" he enquired with an urbane expression – at least, as urbane as he was capable of appearing.

"She's fine, fine. Do you know Coriolan?"

"Ah, good-day to you, sir! My dear Vincent, so you've come with a Spanish friend, have you? Do you never go anywhere alone?"

And he was making fun of me, what's more! I became annoyed.

"Coriolan is my business manager! He has come, at my request, to sort out your delay in paying me."

"Steady on, there, steady on!" said Coriolan with a hearty laugh, but the look in my eye checked him.

Not-a-sou seemed dismayed.

"Business manager? Really. But you know that's a job . . . my dear friend, I'm sorry, your name isn't familiar to me . . . and in this business we all know one another . . . anyway, you need experience, tenacity, and you also need to know what's what and . . ."

"Do I look as though I don't know what's what?" asked Coriolan, in his high-pitched, inquisitorial voice, and I turned away, my mind set completely at rest on the issue of my financial prospects.

On the other hand, I was mentally tearing my hair out about something else: what had I done? Of course, taking Coriolan on as my business manager was a brilliant idea for providing his keep, but what was Laurence going to think? I had just chosen as my agent a man whose total irresponsibility she had been denouncing for the past seven years. In her eyes, this would be a deliberate insult, proof that once again I completely scorned her judgement. She would never believe I had done it on the spur of the moment, without thinking, out of annoyance with Not-a-sou, as well as out of kindness towards Coriolan. She would never believe in any thoughtlessness on my part. (For that matter, people are all the same: forgetfulness, pure and simple forgetfulness, never seems to them sufficient reason for not following their wretched advice.) On the other side of the windowpane, between the rustling chestnut trees in the Champs-Elysées and myself, the indignant, sorrowful face of poor Laurence suddenly interposed itself. I looked away towards Not-a-sou, who was listening, wide-eyed, sunk in his armchair, to what Coriolan was saying.

"There was a client like you at the Neuilly tote: quite simply, he wouldn't pay his debts. That aside, he was a likeable fellow, with a magnificent office in avenue de l'Opéra, a respectable bank account, the lot. Yet he owed five hundred thousand new francs. I had to go out of my way to pay him a visit in avenue de l'Opéra, just as I've come today to the Champs-Elysées. Now, I don't like the 16th arrondissement. So you're going to have to give Vincent what you owe him here and now. Otherwise . . ." (And he leant forward and lowered his voice). I strained my ears in vain.

"But come now . . ." stammered Not-a-sou, "come now, my dear Coriolan, you know about the delays at SACEM?" he said out loud.

Coriolan leant forward again, dismissed SACEM with a wave of his hand, and went on in an undertone with whatever he had been saying. Gradually, Not-a-sou's interruptions became more subdued, and he was whispering when he opened his desk and took out some papers. Coriolan shot me a look of triumph and I returned an enthusiastic smile. Come what might, it was at moments like this that a fellow became once again most appreciative of his friends' virtues.

In short, I was delighted, Coriolan was delighted and, oddly, Not-a-sou seemed relieved. We all three went out to lunch together with a rock group and a famous female singer, who were also clients of Delta Blues. I had a call put through to Laurence to tell her that I would not be home for lunch, my scruples having been overcome by the encouragement and arguments of my two henchmen. They did not threaten me with ridicule, for it was a long time now since I'd had any care for ridicule, but they accused me of meanness: I should pay for lunch, they said firmly. In any case, I was already headed for such marital rows with this idea of Coriolan as my business manager that another two hours would make no difference. I simply told the cloakroom attendant to ring and apologize on my behalf: I knew that if I told Laurence I would not be home for lunch, she would excuse me with one of those indulgent remarks of hers more venomous than any abuse. And I was in a good mood, too good a mood – at the mere sight of Coriolan's eyes, bright, shining and relieved – to tolerate any cloud over my happiness. I too could be selfish now and then . . .

Chapter Two

Two hours later I left Coriolan, scared but arrogant in his new role, to deal on his own with the accountant of Delta Blues Productions, which he persisted in calling "Depression Niçoise". Maybe his own disrespect for money would make him a wonderful agent for others. And besides, I was not planning to tell Laurence of his appointment the moment I got home. I preferred to wait until a stupendous cheque fell into our hands.

It was nearly four o'clock when I quietly pushed open the door to our flat. A melodious tide, a marvellous soaring assailed me: it was the Schumann concerto coming from Laurence's room as though to attack me. For a moment I thought of going to the studio, at the far end of the flat, a room that had been allotted to me for my tune-tapping at the piano, but to get there I had to go through our bedroom, or else walk past Odile, my secretary.

Odile had been at school with my wife and was one of her many admirers, to whom Laurence had entrusted my mail and telephone calls, which were more frequent since my sudden fame. Good-natured, athletic, and plain, Odile was one of those women who get trapped in their "awkward age" and then for the rest of their lives enact, hopefully but ineptly the roles of young girl, young woman, then woman in her prime, etc., etc., without ever managing to convince either themselves or anyone else of the authenticity of their roles. Odile would arrive early, leave late, reply on my behalf to a rather meagre post consisting mostly of requests for money.

Such was, said Laurence, the classic post of a composer of popular hits. Naturally, success as a virtuoso would have brought me more sophisticated post, and brought her a more honorary existence. When a woman has imagined herself dining at Bayreuth or Salzburg with Solti and Caballé after her husband's recital, and she ends up in Monte Carlo for the Eurovision Song Contest, she may be disappointed. When she has imagined this same husband, in tails, on stage, before an enthusiastic audience, and then finds him in the wings, offering encouragement to some squeaky-voiced vocalist who will sell millions of copies of his records, she may be even more disappointed. That said, in the course of seven years, these caricatural images regarding my career ought to have faded somewhat. And after all, what made her think that I myself was not sensitive to the attractions of this romanticism? That she would like to have been Marie d'Agoult did not rule out the possibility that I would like to have been Franz Liszt. After all, I knew the difference between Beethoven and Vincent Scotto. It was no demonstration of kindness or intelligence to be filling my ears from morning till evening with tides of Schumann, like a constant reproach. I would explain all this to her one fine day – some other day, for right now she was bound to be galled by that unexpected lunch with Not-a-sou. And, let me say again, I hated to upset Laurence.

So, judiciously, I went down the corridor to the kitchen, and therefore past Odile's office, to get to my studio. My sanctuary. My refuge. "But what refuge?" Coriolan had exclaimed upon seeing it. "What refuge, since you have to brave two guards in order to retire to it?" He was exaggerating, as usual. I was sure that Odile was well disposed towards me, and prepared to close her eyes to my misdemeanours, if I committed any. I did not know whether she even considered me a good-for-nothing: I had rapidly determined to prove the unfairness of this reputation as a good-for-nothing – a reputation that in the early days of my marriage had wide currency among Laurence's girlfriends (who had generally married into money) – whilst at the same time giving these ladies some of her reasons for marrying me. All this, of course, had been done with the utmost discretion; although there are few men in the circles in which she moved – as in all social circles, unfortunately – who take the least trouble to hide their misconduct, Laurence had never had anything but fears regarding my faithfulness, yet not the least proof of their well-foundedness. I disliked those couples who make it a point of honour to inform each other of their infidelities, under the pretext of honesty; an honesty thoroughly tainted, in my eyes, with sadism or vanity.

"Vincent? Well, I never!" cried Odile in a tone of surprise as though dozens of men habitually went tiptoeing through her office in the middle of the afternoon. "Vincent! Have you seen Laurence?"

"No," I said. "Why do you think I came in this way?"

"But . . . but . . ." The poor girl was at a loss for words, for everything Laurence told her, and her entire posture, made us out to be the perfect couple.

"But she's waiting for you . . . She's waiting for you!" And her eyes, her hands, her voice, her whole body sought to direct me towards Laurence's bedroom, towards Schumann – towards marital bliss and great music, to be more precise.

"I don't want to disturb her," I replied, and rather hastily entered my studio.

I had broken the moral code of this household; I would be punished for it. All the same, I was not going just to stand there with that guilty look I could see myself wearing in the mirror. I took off my raincoat and threw it on the bed before striding out again.

"Ah, there you are . . .!" said Odile, and if she did not add "What a tease!" it was only through lack of conviction.

I winked at her and she blushed. Poor Odile! It would have been an act of charity to make love to her, but I was too selfish for that. All the same I smiled at the thought that Laurence really had chosen as my secretary the ugliest of all her best friends.

I came into the bedroom – our bedroom – whistling: Schumann of course. Laurence was waiting for me in her negligée, in front of a well-stoked fire. And I recalled an autumn evening five years ago when, having been to audition at the Salle Pleyel, I came home humiliated and defeated, feeling, for the first time in my life, that I was a failure. For the first time I no longer saw myself as a young man who could or who might, but as a man who had been unable. And this idea terrified me that evening, weighed me down, brought tears to my eyes. In my despondency I would have avoided Laurence, but she had called out to me as soon as I entered the apartment, and I had come into this room, dark as it was now; as now, with the reflection of the fire on the walls.

"Come here, Vincent!" she had repeated; and abased and weary, I had sat next to her in the dark, averting my face for fear that she would question me about that performance at the Pleyel.

But she had asked no questions. She had removed my jacket, my tie, she had dried my hair with her scarf, all the while kissing me very gently without saying a single word, other than "My darling! My poor darling!" in the same low, tender, maternal voice, the very voice I needed to hear. Ah yes, she had loved me!

Yes, Laurence loved me! And it was for memories such as this that I forgave these little demands of hers, the demands of a spoilt child.

Nor did she make any immediate reference to my lunch that afternoon either. On the contrary, she seemed very cheerful, her eyes were shining. So when she spoke of a surprise, my heart leapt: was she expecting a child? Yet she did not want one, I knew that. Had she been careless? But it had nothing to do with a child, only a parent.

"Guess who telephoned earlier? My father!"

"What's come over him?"

"He's had a heart attack and he considers our row grotesque. He doesn't want to die without seeing me again. He realizes the absurdity of his . . . well, of our quarrel."

"And so, he accepts me!"

I could almost have laughed. What a day! An agent at noon, a father-in-law at five! Life was blooming.

"What do you think of that?"

I looked at her. As far as I could tell from her expression she was moved.

"Well, I think it's made you happy. And that's natural, he's your father."

She gave me a curious look.

"And what if I were horrified?"

"That would be natural too: your father hasn't changed."

My replies seemed to me quite subtle, but Laurence did not appreciate them, which led me to comment on them:

"It's natural that you should be delighted about your parent's change of heart; but since your parent has your father's character, it's natural that . . ."

"Oh, stop it," she said, "please. Your perpetual bantering! By the way, did you enjoy your lunch, with your artists, your musicians – M. Ferdinand Palassous's musicians? Are you still enjoying your new friends?"

Her voice was full of contempt, and for once I rebelled. Since the irruption of this music, of this success, into my life, I felt more sure of myself. I had the agreeable sense of not being a total incompetent. Or rather, the conviction thus far that I was incapable of earning my living had been shaken by the success of "Showers". Of course, this success, as I've already said, might just have been an accident; but, after all, nothing proved that it was. Some musicians tended to believe the contrary, even saw me as a composer with a future. So I replied in a dignified manner:

"My darling, they're my colleagues! So of course I wasn't bored."

She looked at me and burst into sobs. I took her in my arms, amazed. First of all, because I had not often seen Laurence in tears; secondly, because it was never I on those occasions who had provoked them – something of which I was not a little proud. So I gently hugged her, apologizing and murmuring, "My darling! My little darling! Please don't cry! I missed you all the way through the meal", etc., etc. Then, since she continued to sob, I hugged her harder and harder until the physical pain eventually calmed her down. She struggled to free herself and finally broke loose, panting.

"You don't understand," she said, with her hands on her breasts, "it's such a horrid world! You even got the cloak-room attendant to ring me, the way all those guys do, out of cowardice, so that their friends don't get the impression that there's someone waiting for them at home. That bogus freedom, that semi-boorishness! Oh, no! The total mediocrity of those people! How can you?"

And she wept brokenly, choked with sobs, and I admitted she was right. And then the warmth of her tears coursing down my own cheeks, the slight feverishness of her skin, her hair stuck to her forehead, the trembling of her body – all these things made my heart bleed. I was brimming over with compassion, a humane and tender compassion. So I was completely astonished when she slipped her hand under my shirt, took me by the hand and led me to the bed: astonished and disconcerted. After all, she had been full of blame ten minutes ago, in floods of tears three minutes ago, and very probably seething with contempt in the afternoon. How could she now so suddenly desire me? Unfortunately for me, my nature was one of ridiculous straightforwardness; my heart and body had always operated in concert and, in me, desire followed from intimacy, from harmony, as naturally as flight followed from disagreement. No one was further from being a rapist than I, and I had never experienced that divorce between emotional feelings and physical sensations that adds spice to so many stories and gives rise to so much literature. In short, to put it plainly, Laurence's scenes and sulks had always unmanned me. I knew that I was simple-minded and very backward in this respect, and I reproached myself for it as though for some oafishness, but there was nothing I could do about it.

Yet that afternoon Laurence gave herself to me as she had not done so for a long time, a very long time; to the point that some of her cries, some of her gestures seemed to me not only a little forced but addressed to someone else, to a more lyrical, more ardent Vincent whom I regretted not being, whom I was even afraid at one point of betraying, and whom only vanity allowed me to impersonate creditably.

I had tea a little later in the drawing-room, beneath Laurence's ironic gaze. True, I was fully dressed again, whereas she, in a creamy negligée, with her bedroom eyes, left our earlier activities nothing of a mystery. She was accusing me, in an amused voice, of being prudish, and I, in an inaudible voice, was accusing her of being common. The way that more and more couples, these days, make a point of letting others know about their love-making, no sooner is it over: the jovial vanity with which they seem to be inspired by an activity that, after all, any other mammal indulges in with equal enthusiasm and vigour – all this struck me as grotesque and uncalled-for ... Yet even sated love was as nothing compared with impending love! I had observed for myself, and heard it said a hundred times, that those who, by their state of agitation as well as by the fondling they lavish on each other, wish to make us share or guess at their partner's – and their own – very imminent pleasure, often confine themselves to these promises of pleasure. Which was very logical, I thought, impotence being the only explanation for these deliberate and distressing delays inflicted upon their ardour.

To have done with these generalizations: I objected to the spectacle of Laurence, looking radiant and languorous, being served tea by strait-laced, frustrated Odile.

"But," she said, "it's only Odile! There's no one but Odile! You're not ..."

At which point, Odile arrived and sat down, simpering.

"Oh, by the way," I said, "a young girl with green hair asked me, at Delta Blues Productions today, whether I had received her letter. She wrote to me last month, with a request for an autographed photograph, the poor girl! Does that ring any bells with you, Odile?"

To my great surprise she blushed scarlet and it was Laurence who replied briskly:

"You know very well that Odile sorts your mail! To do that, she has to read the whole lot, before passing on to us the most . . . let's say, the least trivial letters. I confess, I haven't had time to go through them recently. I'm to blame for falling behind."

I was initially astounded, then supercilious. Of course it hadn't occurred to me that strangers might write to me, but they had. So I had received letters, Odile and my wife had intercepted them and read them out of curiosity, failing in the end to pass them on to me. Hence that guilty look I saw in them, and which it was now my turn to savour. Not that their behaviour seemed to me so very shocking. Naturally, if I had been expecting love letters I would have found it despicable and I would have yelled at them, but this was not the case and I blamed them just for their cheek. The immorality of an action is only ever apparent to me through its consequences; and I had no intention of pontificating, upholding certain principles – abstract and callous principles – upon which Laurence and her friends based their criticisms of me. Yet here I had a splendid opportunity to rebel, to talk of confidentiality and sigh for the discretion of the past. But I was, as I've already said, incapable of melancholy and bitterness, and even – a more serious matter – of forcing myself to make a show of them. In fact, setting myself in judgement of Laurence seemed to me as futile as vice-versa.

For guilty I clearly was. In the eyes of my father-in-law, for instance, I had always been a good-for-nothing; but so I was in my own eyes. It should have occurred to him that the fact that I had resigned myself to anonymity, and foregone being somebody and earning my living, was due primarily to my artistic temperament. Had I gone into marketing or commerce, I might have deluded us both about myself for much longer than was possible in the music world. Mediocrity is, of course, less obvious in a grocery store than a concert hall. It was out of honesty that I had not spent years furiously banging away at my piano or giving music lessons, which would not have helped matters at all. Painful though this realization had been, it had saved me time, yet without leaving me in any way bitter: I had retained a great appetite for life. And I sometimes wondered whether I owed my steadfastness to my own inner resources (which had served to make this setback endurable in terms of morale) or to Laurence's resources (which had served to make it financially endurable). In fact, it was no doubt due to both.

Odile had gone to fetch some petit-fours, and Laurence, evidently not amused by my mail as the topic of conversation, decided to change the subject.

"That suit looks divine on you!" she said, running her eyes over my body, from the roots of my hair to the tips of my toes. "We were right to take the grey-blue rather than the grey-green, don't you think? It goes much better with the colour of your eyes!"

I nodded gravely. I loved the way she used "we" with regard to my trying on clothes. "We" had chosen this fabric, "we" had decided on the cut, "we" had taken the right shirts, "we" had (in the past) bought cufflinks that went with all my shirts, "we" already had Italian moccasins that could be worn with everything, "we" were going to splash out on a tie with a blue background colour that would be able to take that stripe. And my word, if, after all that, "we" weren't happy, it would be a sorry state of affairs – all these "we"s representing Laurence, except the last, which was me. That said, I had over the last seven years managed to regain control of a few of my male activities: I chose my own cigarettes, for instance, my barber, my sports clubs, etc., etc., and various male gadgets. But with clothes it was pointless to try. It seemed that Laurence in acquiring a young and ardent husband had also acquired a big doll to dress. On this issue, over this right, Laurence would never yield, as I had put up enough of a fight to know. So, year after year, every autumn and sometimes in spring, we would go to "our" tailor, where she would refit me in the most fashionable clothes, rig me out in the latest style, beneath the once sarcastic, but nowadays indifferent, gaze of the same tailor and the same finisher ... of all her suppliers (a generally arrogant lot), the only ones whose disappearance would have caused me genuine consternation.

"Why are you fully dressed again?" she asked. "Because of Odile? You think it would arouse her suspicions?"

"No," I said, "no, let's say ... perhaps unfulfilled desire ..."

Laurence burst out laughing.

"Unfulfilled desire! I think you're very conceited!"

"It's not me she might be yearning for," I replied foolishly. "What I mean is ... well ... it's the two of us together ... our image that ..."

But the damage was done and when Odile came back the subject of those missing letters had long since been eclipsed. I spent a good ten minutes lamenting the treachery of the French language. Once Odile had gone, we remained alone, Laurence and I, as so often in the evening, in recent years. I had no other friend but Coriolan now. As for Laurence's friends, they had become so boring that even she was aware of it and had grown tired of them, which I could not help worrying about for I knew that she was not really cut out for solitude, especially at this moment. This moment, as I looked out of the window on to boulevard Raspail, gleaming in the rain, and those words "unfulfilled desire", mentioned in reference to Odile, now seemed to me to hammer at every door, to throb in every neon sign in Montparnasse with renewed strength and brilliance.

Meanwhile, Laurence had arranged our audiovisual love-nest: she had developed the habit of constructing on the carpet, in front of our television set, what she called our "fortress" – that's to say, a four-sided area marked out by the sofa cushions. There, with me at her side, like some fairy with the aid of her remote-control magic wand, she directed the course of our reveries; switching from one channel to another, from fairy story to documentary, she ruled her little world. And the television being what it is, I would quickly fall asleep, as soon as we had finished our ready-prepared meal from the latest caterer she was using (she changed to a new one every week, and always disastrously).

That evening I was restless. What I heard coming from our TV set seemed even more insufferable than usual, and in spite of myself, my arms and legs kept breaking out of their velvet castle. Especially since Laurence was nestling up closer and closer to me. She was one of those women who make up to you to remind you, beforehand, that you have to make love to them, and who also make up to you, afterwards, to remind that you have done so; which leaves a man with little time to think, and above all prevents him from knowing what stage he is at. Trusting to chance, I took Laurence in my arms and kissed her.

"Oh no!" she said. "What a sex maniac you are! Have you thought about my father? What's your decision?"

"Whatever you've decided."

And she planted a grateful kiss on my cheek. "You've no hard feelings, then?"

"No. I've always thought it terribly petty to bear grudges. Anger, yes! But afterwards, forget it! It's better, don't you think?"

I sincerely hoped she would retain this lesson as an absolute principle, indeed that she would even act upon it.

"How right you are!" she said. "My father would like to see us at his office the day after tomorrow – to see both of us, but to talk to you alone for a while. I think he wants to apologize to you, and it would embarrass him in front of me."

"That's a great shame." I was smiling, but I was quite pleased: it would be easier to make insinuations, to needle him and send him up, if I were on my own rather than in front of Laurence, who was beginning to know me.

"And then you know," she added, "he's a marvellous businessman. Whatever you might make out of your ... those ... that song of yours will give you a bit of pocket money ..." And thereupon she stopped dead, for "pocket money" had become a forbidden expression between us, at any rate a delicate one, since a dinner-party at her lawyer's. The lawyer's wife, after relating the countless villainies committed by her son, had concluded: "And yet I give him so-much pocket money a month!" – the "so-much" corresponding exactly with the monthly allowance that Laurence gave me. I had at once disappeared under the tablecloth, supposedly to recover my napkin – in actual fact, to regain my composure – but as soon I resurfaced, Laurence was able to detect the trace of uncontrollable laughter on my discomposed features. The following month, without saying a word about it, she had exactly doubled my allowance. Why, I don't know. Perhaps because the boy was sixteen and I was thirty-two . . . In any case, for a long time afterwards I blessed that delightful and impecunious young man.

That evening, a little exasperated by Laurence, at the same time sickened by the spectacle on offer on television, and stifled by the velvet cushions, for the first time in a long while I suffered an attack of claustrophobia. Usually, to calm myself, I had only to think of the garret, or indeed the home for young social misfits, where in the normal course of events I should have been living. But that evening I failed. Coriolan's firmness and Not-a-sou's sudden obsequiousness had gone to my head, and all at once I imagined myself coming home to an apartment paid for by me; an apartment where there would be a woman waiting for me, whose life I would share instead of she completely appropriating mine and occasionally tossing me little bits of hers, as she might toss me a bone. On the other hand, the idea of leaving Laurence the moment I had the means to do so seemed to me the lowest of the low. Even admitting that I really had the desire and really had the wherewithal to leave, I had to think seriously about the disgust I would have to live with afterwards: the self-disgust that would certainly be just as strongly felt as the public disapproval, although perhaps not so long-lasting.

Chapter Three

Other people's dreams being rightly considered a terrible bore, I shall confine myself to saying that I dreamed delightful dreams all night long – of snow, piano music, and chestnut trees – but that I awoke feeling even more stifled than usual. The bedroom smelt of perfume and love-making, and despite the dual fascination these exerted over me, already at daybreak I felt as though drugged with them. Fortunately, Laurence had already left, and I opened the window, drew deep breaths of Parisian air, that air, supposedly polluted by petrol and dust, which had always seemed to me the freshest and healthiest in the world. Then I went to the kitchen and made myself a luke-warm Nescafé – for Laurence could not bear the intrusion of a maid in the house before three in the afternoon. I took advantage of this to walk round barefoot on the tiles and carpet, thereby infringing house rules and quietly making the most of the flat. Although big, it was not big enough, I had fast discovered, for an idle man; I was constantly bumping into busy women, and I always ended up taking refuge in my studio, where sometimes I enjoyed being alone. I would have preferred to join in the household routine, to wander round in my dressing-gown and make silly jokes, rather than stay on my own in front of my piano, that broken-winded and cavernous reproach manufactured by Pleyel. It lay idle, thank God, beside a couch, where I always ended up lying down with a book in my hand (I had probably read more in seven years than during my entire adolescence, albeit an adolescence steeped in literature).

I had an arrangement, made the day before, to have lunch with Xavier Bonnat, the director of *Showers*, and his producer. He had asked me to meet him at what had been his favourite restaurant in his days of failure, a place he called his "home", and which was the most squalid place on earth. Despite his recent but unquestionable fame, Xavier still insisted on eating there. Which proved, said Laurence, that success had not gone to his head. Which proved to me that he had definitely gone off his head, for no carnivore could eat in that greasy-spoon café except through starvation and credit combined.

"Home" was a big vaulted room, lit from morning till evening by smoking candles, and with the constant sound of medieval music, replete with reed-pipes, which had a debilitating effect on one's entire nervous system. Xavier Bonnat and his producer, JPS, sat waiting for me at a small table, and I noted that success had not gone to Xavier's head as far as his clothes were concerned either. He still sported the same beige duffle-coat over a greyish-black crewneck sweater. JPS, on the other hand, wore a brand-new suit, which made him look like a real producer at last. Since Xavier Bonnat had a horror of such social pretences, I sat down without shaking his hand and without looking at him. According to Laurence, who had known him since she was sixteen and with whom he had been in love for a long time, Xavier Bonnat was a man who was "all class". A mass of idiosyncrasies, too; tall, thin, with a fine-featured face that people reckoned to be thirty years old, or fifty, although he refused to settle the matter; it turned out he was forty, it was reported in the papers since he had become famous. JPS was the same age, but with a face, a body, a character and apparently a mind that were much more rounded. And he gave me a big smile, which surprised me.

Actually, I was intrigued by this invitation. JPS had been intellectually fascinated by Bonnat since they were at the lycée together, and had since produced every one of Bonnat's films, thereby landing himself with a series of rather expensive flops. This time he had not been able to see the production through to the end and, while the film was still being made, had handed over to professional producers who had relieved him of three-quarters of it. It was these newcomers who, among other changes, had flatly refused to allow Bonnat to use a particularly hermetic piece by Alban Berg to the exclusion of any other music in his film. And it was Laurence who, when he had come complaining to her, had then suggested my name and volunteered my help, which he had jumped at, assuming that, having graduated from the Conservatoire, I was bound to provide him with some serial music (at the very first notes of my more or less melodic score, he had coldly left the editing-room). And the outcome of this story, it seemed to me, was not likely to reconcile our differences: whilst his film had been a success, and attracted some rave reviews, it had also attracted others, including those in his two bibles – that is to say, the *Observateur* and *Cahiers du Cinema*. Coriolan, who hated Bonnat's films, had shown them to me on my return from the Baltic: the former said that without the film's two young actors and, above all, without the music, Xavier Bonnat's images would have appeared even more incoherent in their pretentiousness. As for the latter, why, the reviewer wondered, had such awful images been chosen to illustrate such marvellous music? But still, this had not greatly annoyed Bonnat, or set him against me, apparently, and so much the better.

"What do you think of this success, then?" he asked me.

"Well, you know," I replied cheerfully, "Laurence wanted to see the Baltic islands. We left in the midst of the triumph, and when we got back, it had all calmed down, completely calmed down. But your film's still doing extremely well, I believe," I said hurriedly. "It's jolly good for you," I added, addressing JPS.

"Of course JP would be pleased if he hadn't sold three-quarters of the production half-way through to a bunch of hicks!" said Xavier. "Hicks who could have screwed up the film, what's more, if we'd followed all their diktats!"

Numbering among these diktats myself, shamefaced, I turned to JPS.

"Still, for Xavier, these reviews are marvellous, wonderful, don't you think?"

"I tell you," said Xavier in the same sardonic voice, "I tell you, for once those cold fish deign to open their eyes during the screening of one of my films, and they've not held back. Incredible! Would you . . . wait . . . let me try and remember! Just listen to this! Uh . . . let's see . . . 'Between Lubitsch and Sternberg' . . . 'in short, the combination of charm and seriousness' uh . . . 'a very slight subject requiring a tremendous film-maker to make such a great film of it' . . . no, there's more to come, listen, listen . . . 'Bonnat took every risk and every one paid off, confounding us with delight.' And that's not all, there are even better ones!"

"Wait! Wait!" (This was JPS speaking.) "Wait, there's one that I adore: his colleagues . . . unshaven . . . – you know the one – the . . . clouds!"

"Don't get it all mixed up," Xavier said severely, cutting him short. " 'Unlike his colleagues, Bonnat takes us neither down into the gutter nor up into the clouds: on the razor's edge.' "

"That's it, that's it, on the razor's edge! I think that's terrific! And it's true, what's more, incredibly true!"

"Can you imagine!" continued Bonnat. "And there are others I haven't mentioned . . ."

He still had that sniggering laugh, but in his eyes and in his voice there was a touch of something closer to happiness than derision. I found it hard to imagine that a person could remember so many phrases about himself, out of disgust.

"Mind you," said JPS, "the music really contributed to the film's success, that's undeniable."

"You mean, it's in-dis-pu-ta-ble!" Xavier forcefully concurred.

"Oh," I said, "let's not exaggerate! The music . . . of course . . . but still, it isn't . . ."

Unfortunately, I could not recall the least review as accurately as Xavier. So I assumed an air of modesty, which struck me, after all, as the most seemly in the circumstances.

"I'm very pleased for you!" declared JPS.

"So am I," said Xavier, in a tone of voice that made me instinctively expect an "I suppose" – but he stopped there. "As a matter of fact, I was saying the same thing to Laurence only yesterday."

"You saw Laurence yesterday?"

"I had coffee with her. She told me about the difficulties you're having with your producer . . . that fool Not-a-sou. You've got to do something about it, old man!"

"Two million's not to be left lying in a drawer."

"Two million?" I looked at him. "I was reckoning on about . . . Two million? New francs?"

"Two million dollars. When I talk money, I only talk in dollars," said JPS loftily, tugging on the new waistcoat that was part of his new three-piece suit.

"You mean . . . According to my calculations, Not-a-sou owed me around six hundred . . . well . . . sixty million, old francs, from what I understood . . ."

"Right now he owes you a million dollars, in other words six hundred million old francs, with the same to come from America! I'm not joking," said JPS, "I'm not joking! I had Vlamink's investigate your royalties – he, by the way, is in a different league as a business manager."

I gazed at him, dumbfounded, not so much by these figures (after the first few zeros, one more did not make a great deal of difference in my eyes), as by this consideration of his.

"You had Vlamink's investigate my royalties? That's very kind . . ."

JPS had turned scarlet. Xavier gave him a chilling look, but suddenly started laughing. He had an open, friendly, contagious laugh of which he did not make enough use.

"OK, Vincent," he said, "let's get down to business! I didn't invite you to lunch so that we could quote rave reviews at each other."

I very nearly pointed out that it was his reviews that had been quoted at me, and not the other way round. But it was my fault, after all, I had only to learn some too.

"Nor did I invite you to tell you the state of your finances, although . . . This is the situation: now, you've read the reviews? Well, the person they're calling the Sternberg or the Lubitsch of today can't find a producer for his next film."

"No?"

"Now just a minute! Just a minute! He can't find a producer for *The Wasps*," JPS corrected him.

But Xavier interrrupted him:

"It has been my intention, for a very long time, to make a film of Aristophanes' *The Wasps*. Laurence claims that you read a lot, but all the same, I imagine you won't have read *The Wasps*?"

"That's something I could be accused of . . ."

"It's something many people could be accused of," Xavier conceded indulgently.

"If comes to that, the whole of Paris would be guilty!" added poor JPS. "Don't you understand, no one's read your *Wasps*."

"It's a splendid play about justice and money," declared Xavier, not taking any notice of him. "But I want to film it with unknown actors, on a single set, and in black and white. And I can't find the money to do it."

"That surprises you?" I said, seized with common sense. "It shouldn't surprise you," I went on hurriedly. "Producers being what they are! Imagine: unknown actors, a single set, black and white! Would it be a talking picture?"

They exchanged the same look, half wary, half scornful.

"We can be grateful for small mercies!" groaned JPS. "*The Wasps* is bad enough! Can you imagine *The Wasps* as a silent movie, into the bargain?"

"You mean, without the bzzzz, bzzzz?" I asked with infinite wit, but I was treated to the same look.

Suddenly very serious, Xavier leant across the table.

"There's no question of my not making *The Wasps*! It's vital to me! It may be a matter of pride, of self-esteem, but I must make *The Wasps*, especially after my success!"

"I don't see why," cried JPS, but he fell silent before he

could finish saying what he was thinking, which must have been, "I don't see why you insist on making a turkey after a success." Xavier cut him short.

"Well, I do, you see! So! JP hasn't got the money, would you believe? A quarter of the profits! JP got only a quarter of the profits, and, on top of that, he has to share it with me. However, one-eighth of the money from *Showers* won't pay for the production of *The Wasps*. So I thought of you: let's pool our resources! Let's put together my ideas, JP's experience, your money, and let's make *The Wasps*, as we wish, and without those other people! We'll share the profits, if there are any, between the three of us; just as, in the event, all three of us will share the reviews and the frenzy and the hatred. And when I say hatred, I mean hatred: for it's a strong subject, and a topical one."

I stared at them in astonishment: this was the first time in my life that I was being asked for money, never having had any before. It struck me as a curious concept.

"It's a bold project, a crazy project, it's true," Xavier conceded, "but I think it's worth trying. And I can tell you that Laurence agrees with me! I spoke to her about it yesterday."

"That's just it: I would very much like to pay back Laurence a little of what I owe her . . . I wanted . . ."

"You'll never be able to do that! *Ne-ver!*" Xavier rapped out with great firmness behind a resigned smile. "For as you very well know, what you owe Laurence can't be counted or repaid."

"And besides," JP volunteered, more prosaically, "besides, a million dollars might be enough for the film. You would still be left with as much again to pamper your Laurence. Or whoever you like!" he added with indulgent heartiness.

Xavier shot him another withering glance, and he lowered his eyes.

"I don't think Vincent has got the heart to . . ." and there Xavier stopped, in the face of imaginary and obscene vulgarities. "No, let's talk seriously, Vincent! You know very well that Laurence doesn't want any of that money from

Showers? She doesn't want any of it, she told me so herself."

"I really don't see why . . ." I began, suddenly furious. He cut me short:

"Laurence is such a sensitive creature!"

"Now, when it comes to sensitivity, your wife! . . ." said JPS extravagantly, raising his eyes to heaven, and he nodded several times, as though he might have been a qualified judge of sensitivity.

Since my arrival I had remained slumped limply in my chair, taking it all in. All of a sudden I sat up, put my hands in my pockets and took on a manly voice:

"Let's see now," I said. "To sum up: first of all, if I understand correctly, I'm going to get two or three million dollars; secondly, Laurence, who's too sensitive for that kind of money, doesn't want any of it; thirdly, she agrees, however, that my dollars should finance your next film, based on Aristophanes' *The Wasps* – that's right, isn't it?"

The two lads looked at each other with a kind of doubt that was quite amusing to watch, but which gradually dispersed in the face of the evidence, so that they replied in unison for once, like duettists.

"That's about right, yes!" – in faint voices.

"Only, I don't agree!" I went on. "I'm not too sensitive for that money. So I'm going to spend it fast, and without the help of your *Wasps*. You know what terrifies me about your project? It's that neither of you is going to invest your one-eighth of *Showers* in this *Wasps* of yours! Why not? Not that stupid? Gentlemen, good-day!"

And I left. But I had time to catch JPS's voice, a voice that carried even more because he was whispering, a voice both dismayed and triumphant, saying to Xavier Bonnat: "You see, I told you so! There can't be such a person . . . Such a moron can't possibly exist, it would be too good to be true! And anyway people would know about him . . . I told you so . . ." etc. etc.

Outside on the pavement I burst into laughter, and chuckled to myself for a good two minutes . . . The people I passed smiled at me too. Contrary to what was said, I had always known Parisians to be ready to take the first opportunity to be entertained.

In any event, I personally felt greatly cheered. First of all, by the figures JPS had given me, which were bound to be correct: you could not rely on JPS for anything, except when it came to figures. Moreover, he had seriously applied himself to these, because he had hoped to relieve me of the money; he must have worked it out in detail, to the very last cent. Two or three million dollars! I was as high as a kite. This was something to celebrate and, since Laurence was too sensitive, I would gladly wait a while, for as long as it took before she considered my money respectable – and knowing her as I did, this would not be a matter of years.

I rushed off to an outfitters. Throughout the seven years that Laurence had been dressing me – at one time as a musician of the Romantic period; at another, as a diplomat of the 1930s – I had genuinely longed for a corduroy suit, a little too big and a little baggy. I found one at once. And what's more, it suited me: "The same colour as your hair and your eyes, sir!" cried a sales assistant without any ambiguity this time. I bought an American shirt with a button-down collar, a knitted woollen tie to go with it, and paid for everything with a cheque – a cheque on the account that Laurence had opened for me at her own bank.

It was into this account that she paid a cheque corresponding to my pocket money, on the first of every month; she found this more gracious than giving me cash. It was also out of this account that I settled bills for restaurants, hotels or night-clubs, for all those places, in fact, where what she called my pride, but which in reality was hers, might have taken a knock in public. (I must say, she would reimburse me for these exceptional expenses the very next day.) Of course, it was the end of the month and my account was empty, but Coriolan, drunk with pride, had told me that he had managed to extort a substantial cheque from Not-a-sou the day before, which together we would go to pay into the aforementioned bank. I could already imagine the expression on the manager's face – a decent chap, as it happened, who had shaken my hand as though I had pulled off some amazing deal when my pocket money doubled (in circumstances known to the reader). So, after seven years in which he had seen me invariably spending a small amount of money, three-quarters of it on gourmet meals that were immediately reimbursed, the arrival of these millions was going to make his head swim, perhaps even disappoint him; he couldn't have many clients who were such gourmets on such a modest income.

In the same rush of enthusiasm, I added a raincoat just as I was leaving. And tucking the bag that contained my former livery under my arm (I had already forgotten whether it was a charcoal-grey houndstooth or a pepper-and-salt check), I strode off towards boulevard Raspail. It seemed to me that women were looking at me; I threw back my head, took off my tie and quickened my step. Rather idiotically, I felt master of the city, if not of myself.

Boulevard Raspail, if you turn into it at boulevard Saint-Germain and walk up to the Lion de Belfort, is a long and steady slope that eventually climbs more than a kilometre up the hill of Montparnasse, without too many bad crossings for a pedestrian. Nevertheless, I was out of breath when I reached our block. From rue de Rennes I had seen my reflection in countless shop windows begin to stoop, whilst my suit became a little too young or a little too old – either way, preposterous. I was less sure of myself and less dashing on entering the apartment, but I could tell from a certain quality of silence that Laurence was not at home. Relieved, I headed for my studio, almost prepared to be cowardly and change. The cry that Odile uttered when I came into her office gave me as much of a fright as it did her. She stood behind her desk, staring at me, her eyes popping out of her head.

"Who is it? Who is it? My God, it's you, Vincent! I didn't recognize you at first."

"Because of my suit. I bought it on boulevard Saint-Germain." And holding my arms out sideways, I swivelled round on my heels in order to measure the effect produced.

But I detected nothing but bewilderment in her eyes.

"I've never seen you without a tie," she said. "It's what I'm used to, no doubt, I don't . . ."

"But you've seen me in a dressing-gown before, haven't you?"

"That's different! I've never seen you without a tie, it's not the same thing . . . with a suit, I mean . . . Just then, I thought you were . . . a stranger!"

"You mean that my bare neck suddenly obscured my face from you?"

"No . . . it's just that . . . you were different, you're . . . different . . . you look different. You look more . . . more . . . uh . . . more sporty."

I burst out laughing.

"More sporty? Me? Is that a criticism?"

Her blushes amused me and at the same time irritated me. I wanted a personal opinion from her, a woman's verdict; she might be frustrated or a virgin, but she had to give me that verdict.

"So, come on now, Odile, what about it? Do you think it suits me better than the chiné or the pepper-and-salt three-piece? You prefer me with a tie two inches wide, and of three different shades, under an English collar, eh?"

"I don't know, I don't know! It's not easy to decide," murmured the poor girl, who must have been afraid of betraying her dear, infallible Laurence if she decided in my favour. "How do you expect me to decide all that in a minute?" she groaned.

"I'm quite happy to give you an hour to consider your verdict on my clothes, but that seems a bit pretentious. So choose! What about it now, do you find me more sexy like this?"

"Sexy? More sexy?" She was practically shrieking. "More sexy?" Her voice had become shrill, indignant – it made me laugh, as though the adjective sexy when applied to me was some kind of blasphemy.

"Well, yes, more sexy!" I insisted. "I mean, physically more attractive."

"I know perfectly well what you mean, but I consider it an inappropriate word between ourselves, that's all, Vincent," she declared nobly.

Her voice was scornful, she removed her glasses with a sweep of her hand and since she stood hunched behind her desk, with her back to the wall and her hands clutching her chair, this will to scorn came across very badly. Her lovely eyes, unfocused without her glasses, wandered over me without seeing me, and all of a sudden this exasperated me, made me take two steps forward and kiss her passionately on the mouth. Like any woman who sucks violet-flavoured liquorice from morning till evening, Odile smelt of violets, and this was not at all unpleasant.

"My God!" she said when I released her. "My God!" And she reeled against me.

I righted her, like a child, and smoothed her hair down, quite moved by that scent of violets that reminded me of someone, but who? My grandmother, I feared. This was not the time to be thinking of my grandmother.

"Would you rather I kissed you in my Peter Pan collar?" I asked, refusing to give up.

"But . . . but" – she was whispering, I don't know why – "but," she finally concluded in a distracted manner, "a Peter Pan collar isn't at all what you think. Peter Pan collars are for women!"

I leant forward and continued to kiss her gently, on the nose, on the mouth, on her forehead, on her hair, talking all the while. She smelt good; she smelt of sandalwood soap, the sort you could buy for three francs in chemists; and above all she smelt of violets.

"So," I said, "men don't wear Peter Pan collars. Well, that's rid me of a preconception that was costing me dear. It's delicious, that scent of violets. I could be with my grandmother. That's who it is, I'm sure of it!"

"Your grandmother?" she repeated in a horrified voice, at the same time beginning to return my kisses.

"She also used to suck violet-flavoured sweets," I explained, to reassure her. "Are you kidding – I didn't do anything naughty with my grandmother."

"But we're doing something wrong!" she said in a childish and rather silly voice. "Can you believe it, Vincent? Can you believe it? Laurence is my best friend!"

I gave her one last kiss and straightened up, quite touched and quite enchanted. Wearing this brown suit for the first time had been a decided success. Even though poor Odile was not at all pretty, she had a gentleness about her, when you kissed her, a shamelessness, that was worth six pretty little bimbos!

"You must promise me not to do it again," she said, lowering her eyes.

"That I can't promise you!" I replied with all the politeness in the world. "But I'll try, I promise you, I'll try! Come on, now, you know full well, Odile, that I love Laurence, that she's my wife, that she's my spouse, you know the ties that bind us!"

I had gone through to my studio and I was trying to get rid of the totally indelible lipstick she had put on my mouth. Looking at myself, I no longer felt sympathy but compassion for this tanned, dark-haired fellow – "Your colours, sir!" – for this stranger who was so distant from me, and so close, with whom I slept a great deal and lived so little, with whom I often had fun but to whom I never spoke. I barely heard Odile's reply.

"You're right, Vincent, Laurence is a wonderful person and . . ."

I went to the piano and punctuated each of my phrases with a chord of A sharp, F, and D minor that I had just discovered, and which was superb.

"I'll have you know, Odile, that I respect my wife! [Chord] And that I respect her home! [Another chord] And that I admire her, Odile! [Chord] That I revere her, that I am madly devoted to her, Odile! [Chord] I've always been devoted to her, as you know, Odile!" I said, playing another two chords and I very nearly fell over backwards when I heard Laurence's voice, a cheerful voice, calling out from the next room:

"What a delightful homecoming for a woman! Why don't you make your declaration to me, my dear, instead of bothering Odile?"

I very quietly played one last chord on my piano, by way of thanking fate, and emerged looking like a man caught being blatantly sentimental. I felt meek and foolish, and I jumped when Laurence's voice, a totally different voice, lashed out at me:

"Xavier decided to get you to play Al Capone, or what?"

I had completely forgotten my new suit. I bowed my head to look at it again, but Laurence was already turning theatrically to her poor secretary:

"Have you seen how Vincent is dressed, Odile? Am I dreaming or . . . Have you seen him?"

"I've already shown Odile my new suit," I said grudgingly, and I saw Odile flush scarlet. "But I didn't manage to get an opinion out of her."

"It wasn't worth bothering Odile with such horrors," she declared. "Your suit is hideous, my poor friend. Hideous and vulgar! Where could you have bought it? It's out of this world! However, if you like it, you can keep it!"

And turning her back like a fury, Laurence left the room. I shrugged my shoulders and turned to Odile, who looked crushed.

"Actually, I might have had time to change if I hadn't been too absorbed in something else. But believe me, dear Odile, I've no regrets."

I had intoned these words in a dramatic voice and I saw her smile despite herself, a ghost of a smile beneath her lipstick, which she had hastily put on again and which I now realized was vermilion. A ghastly vermilion! What could have prompted me to kiss this flat-chested girl with that vermilion lipstick and those wild eyes? I had some funny ideas sometimes, ideas that I rarely regretted. For me, Odile would, from now on, be linked with a charming taste of violets; and there would always be between us, from now on, that stock of affection shared by two people who have kissed each other in secret. She must have felt this too, since she blurted out in a discreet, low voice, just as I was leaving the room:

"You know, Vincent, really, that suit looks very good on you . . ."

Chapter Four

If I actually preferred wearing that gear, why not stop shaving as well? Why not buy a yellow T-shirt, right away, to match that jacket? And why, if I liked pockets on the knees of my trousers so much, did I not go and kneel outside church doors, with a beret in the same colour, and beg? This was apparently the only use imaginable for that suit of mine!

I raised my hand.

"There are other uses imaginable for everything that relates to me," I said, "if Xavier Bonnat is to be believed."

But Laurence was in full flow and did not hear me straightaway.

"Why not dress exactly like all those other show-business morons? Why . . .?"

She did eventually pause.

"Xavier Bonnat? What's Xavier Bonnat got to do with all this? Don't tell me he has the same tailor?"

During periods of tension between us, Laurence had the habit of addressing me formally as *vous*, a conjugation that, naturally, I adopted when she did, and that similarly I abandoned as soon as she returned to the usual, familiar *tu* once her feelings towards me improved.

"No," I said, "but he put some proposals to me that, I gather, you took it upon yourself to accept."

Laurence shook her head and her long black hair whistled round her face like the amazons' lasso, but she seemed much less at ease, in her little drawing-room, than those wild creatures in their vast territories.

"What are you talking about? Oh yes? He asked me if you would reinvest the profits of that song of yours in his next film, in *The Flies* by Aristophanes."

"*The Wasps*."

"I said that I actually thought it was a good idea," Laurence went on, "but that it was entirely up to you, that the money was all yours, no one else's but yours."

She had assumed that half-inattentive, half-cutting manner that dishonesty gave her.

She carried on:

"I had thought till now that your money was mine, just as mine was yours, that we shared everything! Forgive my naïveté, Vincent . . ." And she turned away in a dramatic movement.

"Oh, come on," I cried. "You know very well that everything that belongs to you, belongs to me . . . No, sorry, it's the other way round . . . I meant to say the opposite, honestly! Only, the fact that everything that belongs to me belongs to you, and vice versa, doesn't mean that everything that belongs to us belongs to Xavier or JPS!"

"JPS?" she said. "Who's that?"

"Sardal, Xavier's producer." And I burst out laughing in spite of myself, at the thought of the expression on Sardal's face while Xavier was talking about Aristophanes. "He's the poor guy who's supposed to produce *The Wasps*, in black and white, with an unknown cast, and probably in the depths of the Massif Central. Can you imagine it?"

Laurence was not laughing.

"Yes, I can. It's a great pity you haven't read *The Wasps*," she said coldly, "because it's a very fine work . . ."

There was a well-established convention between the two of us, alone and in public: just as music was supposed to be my domain, so literature was hers. Unfortunately, I had read a great deal more (at the lycée and during my military service, as well as at boulevard Raspail) than Laurence had ever had the time to read. I had spent fifteen years of my life devouring literature, good or bad, but devouring it. This did not alter the fact that at the dinner-table, whether in private or not, I had to feign ignorance just as often as Laurence had to pretend to be knowledgeable. Had the occasion arisen, I would have bet everything she possessed that she knew absolutely nothing about Aristophanes – whereas I could remember a fair amount about his period, his contemporaries and some of the characters in his plays, and, although very vaguely, even the theme of *The Wasps*. I decided to have a little fun.

"I know that the theme of *The Wasps* is remorse, I know that it has often been taken up by others, notably by the existentialists, that's right, isn't it?"

"The existentialists among others, yes," said Laurence drily. "It was taken up by everyone, the Romantics too, of course."

"All right, let's say that Xavier has had a good idea! Even so, he should have told you that it wasn't three francs I was going to get but three million dollars! He should have been more honest, with you and with me! Anyway, he's so contemptuous, as though he'd like to spit in my face . . . I don't fancy handing over my royalties to a guy so ready to knock me for six . . . I just can't get enthusiastic about it . . . We've all got our own funny little ways . . ."

Laurence was not listening, she look worried: she was obviously wondering where she had put the Encyclopedia of Literature, so that she could look up under W this famous play of Aristophanes. She responded even more coldly:

"Listen," she said. "Do what you like, Vincent, I've already said, I shan't touch your royalties. I would gladly have shared the results of your work, your genius, your earnings as a virtuoso, but this, a hyped-up show-biz gimmick, a fluke – certainly not. I just can't! Carry on buying your horrible clothes! Or else do something intelligent – like financing *The Flies*, for instance – and then we'll see."

"*The Wasps*," I automatically corrected her.

"*The Wasps*, if it matters so much to you!" In her annoyance she had reverted to using *tu*, and I started to laugh.

"It mattered to Aristophanes. Just think how tedious it must have been for him in his day, poor man, to have to keep correcting people each time they said flies instead of wasps."

"Why? Why each time?"

"Because, my darling," I said, "there were no wasps at that time in Greece, there were only flies, not a single wasp! The wasp was the symbol of remorse, and Aristophanes' heroes, as you know, feel no remorse. Just as in Europe cart-horses are a symbol of labour. Yet, you have to admit, you never see any. In any case, I personally have never seen one." I had spoken curtly, and she, her attention caught, took it meekly, even nodded. I was delighted.

Meanwhile, I had to rid her of that disastrous notion of making a film with Bonnat. For I knew that, if I did not, I would be treated to some pointed remarks, even reproaches: either the film would be a success and I should have taken a share in it; or else it would be a failure and if I had shown a little more generosity, it might have worked. In any case, I had to launch a devastating attack against Bonnat himself in Laurence's mind.

"You know, I had a peculiar time with Xavier. He's a strange fellow . . . Do you know him well?"

"Quite well, yes . . ." Laurence had assumed that absent-minded, mellow look that women have when you talk to them about men who have loved them, men they punished by not returning that love – severely punished, even – and to whom they showed not one-tenth of the affection they display now, twenty years later, when invoking their memory.

"Poor Xavier!" she said. "Such a sentimental man . . . But strange in what way?"

"Well, he can't forgive himself for not having snatched you away from me, the gigolo. He says that if he'd made up his mind faster, if he hadn't backed down at the last minute, he might have succeeded. I was furious!"

"What?" she said. "What?" Indignation had wrung a kind of groan out of her. "Made up his mind in time? What does he mean by that? Xavier? He spent five years chasing me, trailing along after me. How can he talk about making up his mind in time? Really? So Xavier let me marry you?" In her annoyance, she was hopping from one foot to the other, and had reverted to using *tu*. "Xavier! Make up his mind earlier!" she doggedly repeated. "Xavier, under my feet from morning till evening, for months, moaning and whining! No, it's incredible! It's unbelievable! He said all that to you, did he?"

I wore an expression at once inscrutable and loyal, the two things being, oddly, quite compatible.

"No, I shan't say anything more. I may have misunderstood him. Anyway, what's so bad about him talking of your love rather than his?"

"But it is bad," she cried in indignation, "it is!"

"He's jealous, that's all."

"But he's not jealous of you," screeched Laurence, all of a sudden furious, "he's not jealous of you, he's jealous of you living the life of Riley, as he calls it! That's what he wants, that's all, honestly! And since he's squalidly tight with money, even your pocket handkerchiefs are a sore point. It stops there, truly, I swear to you it does!"

I loved to see Laurence like this: unrestrained, her voice unrestrained and her face almost common, furious. I adored seeing her like this: cynical, angry, uninhibited, hard; as she refused to see herself, and as she refused to appear. She saw herself as she wanted to be: perfect, spiritual, detached, intellectual, erudite, innocent, dreamy, etc. In short, she wanted to believe herself, and wanted others to believe her, to be the opposite of what she was. And this is one of the great tragedies of the human race, and one of the most widespread, it seemed to me: this negation of oneself, this passion for one's antithesis, a passion carefully concealed and ever renewed; a passion that could not become fierce and dangerous unless it were really one's entire being that was called into question – not, as in my case, a small point of detail. For in my case, I simply wanted to appear a little more serious or hard-working, a little less frivolous and absent-minded, a little more of this, a little less of that. But that was all: I did not see in myself any fault or quality so obvious or so unpleasant that I should wish for the exact opposite. Truly not: either through laziness or what was, after all, a creditable modesty.

We both came out of this confrontation exhausted – much more so by the questions we had not put to each other than by those that had arisen of themselves and from outside. I went off to change, to take off my suit and put on a lavallière collar again. And I started chuckling to myself, recalling that moment in the discussion when I had instructed Laurence on the life of insects and the absence of wasps in Aristophanes' day: it would lead to a fine set-to in the near future between her and that wretched Xavier Bonnat. I looked forward to it, even though I would not be there to witness it.

Chapter Five

It was past three o'clock and we were supposed to be at my father-in-law's at four; but Coriolan had just called me and said on the phone: "I must see you right away." So, without telling anyone, I had hurtled downstairs and dashed over to the Lion de Belfort. Coriolan was waiting for me and almost threw himself into my arms. Two sentiments, both extremely rare in a Spanish nobleman, alternated on his face: satisfaction and terror. Eventually he drew from his pocket a cheque for one hundred thousand francs made out in my name and signed by Delta Blues Productions.

"Can you believe it?" he cried. "Can you believe it? He's owed you the money for months, the bastard! On the off-chance, I went back to his place yesterday evening, yelling and shouting, and he gave me this! What are we going to do with it, for God's sake?" he said, darting panic-stricken glances around him.

"Listen, we're not going to bury it in the ground here: you go and pay it into the bank. The chap behind the counter will be delighted. Here, let me write another cheque, made out to you. Get a bit of cash and leave it in an envelope with the concierge at boulevard Raspail. I have to go over to my father-in-law's and Laurence is probably looking everywhere for me. I'll call you later."

"Wait, wait," cried Coriolan. "You have to sign this cheque, on the back."

So I rapidly signed it and drove home. By one of those

strokes of good luck that fate sometimes dispenses, I ran into Laurence, all smiles, on the stairs.

"I was sure that you were warming up the car!" she said, amused. "I told Odile, who was looking for you under your piano, that's where you'd be."

"The thing is, that car goes so well, I'd never forgive myself if I damaged it."

"What a child you are! However, a child that looks after his toys – that's a blessing, at least . . ."

"You ought to tell your father that, to soften him up: Vincent takes very good care of his toys."

Laurence laughed. The car, nicely warmed up, started immediately, and we sped off towards Porte d'Auteuil. At a red light, Laurence inspected me from top to toe.

"You look much better like that," she said, for I had put on her favourite suit – dark blue, with one grey thread in four – and a tie in the same grey, with a blue stripe – the same blue as the suit, of course. In short, taking a sanguine view, I looked like an only very recently successful, young Italian industrialist. That said, after seven years, the looks people gave me no longer bothered me, and yet I had suffered in the past. I had suffered horribly at "my" – or rather "our" – first fitting: Laurence had taken care of everything except my masculine pride, but since she also took care of the bill, I had not remained cross for too long.

Her father's private house overlooking the Bois de Boulogne was a 1930s-style building. He had filled its big, cold, rectangular rooms (and, as he said himself, not so much out of any aesthetic concern as for investment purposes) with a set of Louis XV furniture that, according to Coriolan, was nearly all genuine – and Coriolan was as much an expert on furniture as he was on music. It was as a witness, my witness, that he had attended my wedding and was able to pursue his investigation of this private house; he had been found in the evening, dead drunk, in one of the guest-rooms, with a maid. This had completely discredited him in the eyes of my family-in-law for whom, clearly, it would have been less scandalous to find him in the arms of a young girl, however, much under-age, but from a good family. Incensed by this, I too had become a pariah that same day, and it was the sobs of my mother-in-law that prevented her only daughter's wedding from ending up at the police station.

The door was opened to us by a stranger, dressed as a butler, and curiously this surprised me less than it did Laurence, who immediately cried out anxiously:

"But what's happened to Thomas?"

"Thomas died, madame, two years ago. Alas!" said the butler, bowing sorrowfully, and Laurence's hand tightened on my arm.

"Poor Thomas . . ." she murmured. "Dear, dear old Thomas!" and she gave me a sideways look, a look of sadness.

I blinked twice, mournfully. But a joyful and virile voice made us look up: my father-in-law was coming down the marble staircase in front of us, his hand hovering over the rail. He came to a halt on the next-to-last step, for he was a great deal shorter than me, which irritated him immensely; and we went up to him. Meanwhile, we had exchanged the same look as eight years ago at the time of our brief encounters, the look two people give each other when suddenly confronted with a caricature: for him, the caricature of a useless idle bum, and for me, that of a jumped-up rich bastard. After this instant of mutual recognition, we exchanged a friendly smile, and with her usual grace Laurence took each of us by the arm. She made us shake hands: I shook my father-in-law's hand and he shook mine, over-enthusiastically. We even shook each other's arm two or three times, unnecessarily, and we parted without having attempted the slightest wrench.

"Well! Let's go and drink to this!" my father-in-law proposed with bonhomie, and he directed us into what he called the "bar", the most cheerful room in the house, he said, where indeed the Louis XV armchairs were replaced by more comfortable, leather club-chairs. Once the butler had closed the door again behind him, Laurence said to her father:

"But papa, I had no idea: poor Thomas! What happened to him?"

"What happened was that good old Thomas died! Some wretched business with his kidneys. From one day to the next, he couldn't even carry a tray, poor fellow! But Simon is very, very, very good!" he reassuringly informed us.

And upon that funeral oration, we sat down. My father-in-law eyed me with the same incredulity that he inspired in me. He made an effort:

"Incredible!" he cried. "Seven years already! You haven't changed a bit, my dears! Congratulations!"

"It's the happiness," said Laurence, and she lowered her eyes.

"And the peace and quiet," I added.

I saw my father-in-law turn purple; Laurence had not heard or not understood.

"You know, you look very healthy too, father! I was afraid, after what happened, that you might be . . ."

"I'm made of iron," he said. "And for business, you have to be, believe me! It's no joke on the Paris market, right now. It's a constant battle. I'm very glad you've been spared all that, my dear fellow," he added, turning to me.

"So am I!" I replied in all honesty, and it was he who lowered his eyes.

The butler came back with a bottle of champagne and he served it to us while my father-in-law fidgeted nervously. As soon as Simon was out of the room, he blurted out to Laurence:

"Darling, would you mind leaving us? I must have a man-to-man chat with your husband."

Laurence rose with a smile.

"All right, but be good, both of you! Don't argue. I don't want to hear any raised voices from the other side of this door."

She turned in the doorway to smile at us, and she even blew a kiss into the air, which wavered between us, then flew off elsewhere with all possible speed. I settled back in my armchair whilst my father-in-law started pacing up and down in front of the bar, as he liked to do. Unfortunately, his shoes were too new and squeaked a little, particularly when he turned round.

"My daughter must have told you that I had some heart trouble?" I nodded. "A malformation of the aorta – a common problem but risky."

He spoke of it as he might have mentioned a military medal, with a sombre pride in which there was mingled a trace of emotion. I sensed him waver between getting sentimental with me over his health or continuing to be disagreeable. I helped him make his choice:

"Laurence told me of a malformation but without really wanting to specify where," I said, and I assumed an indulgent and embarrassed look that irritated my interlocuter.

"Of the aorta! Of the heart! I very nearly died!" He checked himself. "I realized then that I was very sorry, yes, very sorry . . ." And he threw out his chest and emphasized each word, with a look of delight. ". . . that I was truly very sorry for having been too hard on you."

"Oh, let's forget all that!" I cried. "Let's forget all that, what does it matter! I never held it against you, you know. Laurence will be so happy . . ."

I rose. This time he lost his temper.

"I haven't finished, young man."

"Vincent!" I curtly corrected him. "It's better that you call me Vincent."

He reared up at this, turned red, even rose on his toes.

"Better? Well, well, fancy that! And why, may I ask?"

"Because it's my name and, alas, I'm not a young man any more!"

"I see!" He dropped back on to his heels. "Well, now, Vincent," he said slowly. "My dear Vincent" – he hesitated, as though prefacing this name he so disliked with an affectionate adjective made him uneasy – "my dear Vincent," he went on just as suspiciously, like someone sucking an unfamiliar sweet. "The two of us need to have a talk, a serious talk. Make yourself comfortable."

"I'm very comfortable. May I smoke?"

"But of course, of course! My dear Vincent" – he was more at ease now, the sweet was turning out to be bitter but edible – "you are not unaware of the reasons for my being hard at the time. I knew that you were talented, and I wanted you to apply yourself. I found it heartbreaking to see you spending your time with my daughter squandering her dowry. For it's all gone, you know . . . Laurence is bankrupt."

"Bankrupt?" I said. "Oh well, never mind! You know perfectly well I didn't marry Laurence for her money . . ."

He was lying in his teeth, for Laurence had a broker whose stentorian tones reverberated at boulevard Raspail every quarter and always ended on a note of triumph. Moreover, I knew full well that, had Laurence been bankrupt, she would have been in a far greater state of panic.

He eyed me warily.

"I know," he said half-heartedly, "as a matter of fact, that's why I let the two of you get married. But I was unaware that one day you'd be able to prove it to her."

I played dumb. He leaned forward.

"I've read the papers, old boy! I've even seen your film. I've heard your music! For that matter, there's no way to avoid hearing it! I must confess, I don't know much about the cinema, and, well, it's the same with music! Only . . . only . . ." He was jovial and almost affectionate. ". . . only I'm going to tell you something, young man: I don't particularly like music, but if a piece of music earns me one million dollars, well, that makes me a music-lover! Hi! Hi! Ha! Ha! Ha! Ha!" he cried. And as he guffawed, he gave me hearty slaps on the back. And I guffawed with him.

In one respect, I was delighted. I tried to remember everything he said so that I could repeat it word for word to Coriolan. For, sadly, I wouldn't be able to repeat it to Laurence. There were few jokes that I could repeat to Laurence; her sense of humour was too different from mine. To be more precise, I could not detect hers and mine irritated her. So on the one hand I was delighted, but on the other hand rather surprised: if my poverty had sown ferment seven years earlier, it seemed that my present wealth was causing even more of a stir.

"Well, then," he said abruptly, catching me off-guard with another slap on the back, which, farcically, made me well and truly splutter on my champagne. "This is going to change your life, eh? Because I know my daughter! It couldn't have been any fun, eh, pocket money, with her?" (A third slap set me to rights again, coughing and sniffling like an idiot.) "Between you and me, the little ladies of Paris are hard to get when you're completely penniless. Ah, if I were your age, old boy! Dear, dear! Hah, I envy you, old boy!" He was about to land me another slap on the back, still man to man. I stepped aside, just in time, and he struck the bar, yet without losing his temper.

"But . . ." I mumbled, "hmmm," coughing nervously, "but what little ladies? You surely don't think I'm unfaithful to Laurence?"

He erupted with laughter, a coarse, wily, wicked laugh that filled me with horror. Yes, I suddenly felt horrified at having been so blithe in bed with my wife's snobbish girlfriends.

"I assure you . . ." I said. But to my great surprise, anger muffled my voice and changed my intonations. All of a sudden my voice sounded like that of a little girl, and I fell silent.

"Not me, old man! Not me!" exclaimed my father-in-law. "Not me! Laurence is just like her mother: she's beautiful, she's intelligent, she's elegant, she's attractive, she's a lady (she's my daughter!), but she's no fun. Ah, my dear friend, my life would have been no joke, at home, if I hadn't been able to look out for myself. Only, I did manage to look out for myself. One day when we're alone, I'll tell you the whole story!"

In the glee inspired by his risqué recollections, or in his exhilaration at the thought of these new millions, he had loosened his collar and tie.

"I'm going to tell you something: when I heard about all this – this lucky break of yours – I thought, there are two alternatives: either the boy stays with my daughter, or else he takes off with the money and some dumb blonde. Let's wait and see . . ."

"You're joking, I hope!" My voice was outraged. "I loathe dumb blondes."

"Ha! Ha! Ha! Ha! Ha! Ha! Thank God, you stayed. Mind you, you wouldn't have got far: because I'm Laurence's father. And when you were married, I made sure she had a cast-iron contract! Your marriage settlement is based on joint ownership of acquisitions made during married life, old boy! Do you know what that means?"

"No, no . . ."

I viewed him with a mixture of amusement and revulsion: seven years ago, despite all his contempt for me, despite his hate-filled certainty that I was the pillager, this man had retained a small hope of seeing me eventually become the pillaged – it was an idea that seemed to me fantastic. Balzacian . . .

"Well, then," I said, "what does it mean?"

He laughed and put his arm round my shoulders.

"It means, old boy, that everything you might have acquired with Laurence over the past seven years is to be shared between you, that's all! There now! It means that you don't owe her anything, if you like, but she must have half of everything you've earned."

I shrugged my shoulders.

"Since I'd made up my mind to give it all to her . . ."

He took me by the arm and whispered:

"Now, that would be a foolish mistake! My dear fellow, there's only one thing to do: you open a joint account, requiring both signatures. Let me explain: Laurence doesn't want any of your filthy lucre, God knows why! She saw you as a pianist! I told her: first of all, my girl, each to his own taste. Personally, I've always preferred Line Renaud to Bach. That's my affair, eh? Secondly, your husband earned that money; it's his! So? Eh?"

I stared at him, slightly appalled. I was beginning to think that we were alike in one respect, and one only – our common sense – and that this was possibly the worst thing.

"Thirdly, with this joint account, she can't draw anything on it directly. If she wants to write out a cheque, you have to countersign it: after all, it's your money! Good! (Obviously, when you withdraw your money, she has to countersign as well, a mere formality!) But for example, if she wakes up one fine day and wants to put her money, that's to say half of yours, in one of those preposterous intellectual films: impossible without your signature . . . That gives you time to dissuade her. You understand? I can't help it, eh, she may be my daughter but in this instance it's you I stand by, for I've no time, myself, for people who despise money! When you think of all the poor devils without it, and so on and so forth . . ."

I stopped listening, but I must confess that something in his reasoning greatly amused me: the idea of Laurence going up to the counter and asking for some cash, and being refused it by a bank clerk requiring my signature on the cheque, struck me, I don't know why, as an idyllic vision.

Eventually my father-in-law called in Laurence, in a needlessly thundering voice for she was behind the door. They argued a bit and we ended up by going straight to the bank. I followed them, gave countless signatures, but not one that was not matched by Laurence (which reassured me) – I laughing, and she sulking. These bankers were past masters when it came to bowing and scraping, and I had a lot of fun.

I had a lot of fun, but once again I shouldn't have taken it so lightly.

We had gone into that bank at five o'clock, and we came out much later, despite the rigid timetables I had thought such establishments kept. It was nearly eight when we got back to boulevard Raspail. Laurence had not said a word throughout the journey, indeed not for a long time: not since our arrival at the bank, in fact, and if her imagination was running along the same lines as mine, I could well understand her.

The little scene I had imagined a short time ago, of

Laurence being turned away by a cashier, had come on considerably in my mind: to begin with, she would arrive in her Chanel suit (an extravagance but it would never go out of fashion), she would push open the electronically controlled door of this bank with an irritated gesture, and walk straight up to "her" teller. Like many people, Laurence had "her" teller, "her" hairdresser, "her" manicurist, "her" lawyer, "her" tax man, "her" solicitor, "her" legal adviser, "her" dentist, etc. Few occupations – taxi drivers, waiters in cafés, and for these people I had developed a certain admiration – escaped this frenetic and silent possessiveness. (As for myself, I have to say I had no one serving under my flag: "my" tailor was chosen by Laurence, the owner of the Lion de Belfort truly ruled the Lion de Belfort, the dentist I had visited twice in seven years was Laurence's etc. etc., right down to the concierge, whom I called "the" concierge, or whom I might, at the very most, have dubbed "our" concierge if Laurence had not always called her "my" concierge in a totally peremptory manner.) When by chance she was obliged to share one of her serfs with a friend, the hairdresser, for instance, or the shoemaker, she would then revert, as co-proprietor, to their family name: "my" hairdresser and "my" shoemaker went back to being Monsieur Hulot and Monsieur Perrin. As a matter of fact, I found this little monarchical habit quite understandable: habit is one of the worst and most insidious forms of possessiveness – in any case, it was for Laurence.

So I imagined her in her Chanel suit, entering the bank, heading for her clerk with her usual determination, and saying to him: "How are you, Monsieur Barras? I'd like some cash, please, I'm in a very great hurry." For there are also places or occupations that immediately provoke haste in their clients (banks, beauty salons, garages, not to mention department stores, which set one off at a positive gallop). "Certainly," would say Monsieur Barras, the bank clerk, whom I had once met: he was a pale man, quite tall, clean-shaven, with glasses and a sort of malicious look about him. "Certainly, my dear Mademoiselle Chat— . . .

Madame Ferzac," he would say, correcting himself, as though, carried away by her appearance, he had almost called her by her maiden name. "How would you like the money?"

"In 500s!"

Meanwhile, Laurence would have opened her bag, removed her glove, taken out her chequebook – "our" cheque book – and hastily scribbled out "three thousand francs", then signed her name with a nervous, high-speed gesture. I don't know why, the grandest people – and the least grand – sign their cheques as though their pen was on fire, as though any slowness in signing was a symptom of obscurantism or total illiteracy. In short, Laurence would sign her cheque and imperiously hand it to the clerk, crouched behind his grille, already eager to demonstrate his alacrity and efficiency. So he would take the cheque, give it a passing glance (if that – an unnecessary precaution, of course, with the lovely Madame Ferzac). And then, lo and behold, if he didn't stop and cast an incredulous look at Laurence, who too froze, her eyebrows raised in enquiry: what was the matter?

"What's the matter?" she would ask him in an haughty and irritated voice. "What's the matter? Could it be that I haven't any money left in this bank?" And she would give an incredulous, indeed sarcastic, little laugh in the face of this, thank God, totally improbable eventuality.

"Of course not, it isn't that, Madame Ferzac." The cashier too would be smiling. "It's simply that, as you know . . . it's a joint account and I'm afraid that both . . ."

"That what? Yes, that what?"

Laurence would lose her temper, drum her fingers on the wooden counter, while the cashier spread his hands in despair:

"Madame, I'm sorry, I'm terribly sorry . . . but, you see, it's a special account, as you know, and we need Monsieur Ferzac's signature."

Laurence would stand there, aghast.

"Monsieur Ferzac's signature? The signature of my

husband, you mean? On my cheques? And for three thousand francs?"

"Madame Ferzac, it's not the amount that matters, it's the principle, as you know . . ."

"No, I know nothing of the kind! In all events, I was unaware that I needed my husband's signature to draw my money! Indeed, I find it insane," etc. etc.

I exulted at the picture of Laurence, bright red in her bright-pink suit, confronting the red-haired clerk, and the manager turning up, purple with embarrassment – in short, a sublime study of fury and dignity. But my wild imagination had made me forget, or rather delay, my discussion with Laurence: I absolutely had to reassure her, to lay her anxieties to rest and soothe her perhaps already wounded pride.

Hardly had we stepped into the apartment when she rushed off to her bedroom.

"My God, it's Thursday the 4th! It's the day of my bridge game! Excuse me!"

She was running away. I caught her by the arm and detained her for a moment, but she turned to face me, eyes shining, and looking extremely pale.

"My darling," I said in a comforting voice, "you surely don't think I'm going to honour that contract with the bank?"

She gazed at me wide-eyed:

"I don't see how you can do otherwise!"

With a laugh, I released her, but after casting me a cold glance she went into her bedroom and three-quarters closed the door. So it was without being able to see her that I was obliged to talk to her.

"You don't really know me. Or rather you don't know me as a rich man. I'm no longer the same person. People change when they become rich!"

"I don't care!" Her voice was cold. "I don't care! I've already made it clear to you that I didn't want a sou of your money. And besides, I don't see how you can change that contract one iota!"

She was absolutely furious and she had cause to be, after all: for a woman who had kept me for seven years, to find herself landed with a potential churl was a rather bitter experience.

"Really, darling, come, now, it's me, Vincent, talking. Listen. Tomorrow I'm going to go to the bank and you'll see that the whole thing's nothing but a joke. Believe me, they'll do what I want."

"I'd be surprised if you can persuade them."

I knew that I would have no difficulty in convincing them to put everything into Laurence's account, which would be the simplest and, after all, the most natural thing to do. I would just get her to sign a cheque to pay Coriolan a lump sum, explaining to her the reason for it – or not – and I would still be left with my royalties on the sheet music, which I had not mentioned earlier at the bank, plus the one hundred thousand francs Coriolan had extracted from Not-a-sou: it wasn't so bad!

"What do you bet?" I said. "You bet that tomorrow you'll go and write your little cheques out again, all on your own, as usual, and that you'll do without my signature?"

There was a silence.

"But you'll need mine," she snapped, as she emerged from the bedroom.

In two minutes she had reapplied her make-up and was dressed in black: she looked like the statue of justice and wrath, which suited her very well, and came as a welcome change from her perpetual flirtatiousness. I took a step towards her, but she promptly backed away, even raised her arm over her face in a defensive gesture that astounded me. I had never struck Laurence, nor even thought of doing so.

"I'm late," she hissed. "Let me go! Can't you see I'm late?"

True enough, every first Thursday of the month, she went to play bridge with her old girl-friends from college, a game by the end of which she would win or lose one hundred francs at the outside; this mad haste surprised me.

"Well, go then," I said, "go! Please don't stake our joint account on a grand slam!"

She was already opening the door, disregarding the lift to start trotting down the stairs. I leant over the banister to watch her descend. She looked up, but not before she had reached the downstairs landing, and with flashing eyes she called out to me in a voice all of a sudden much lighter:

"Can you explain to me how you're going to bring those bankers to heel tomorrow?"

The question was sarcastic. She was being all hoity-toity, but I knew that she would eventually develop an attachment to this money that was so distasteful to her today. Laurence had never spurned money for very long.

"What am I going to do?" I called back, leaning over the rail. "Darling, I'm going to put all those dollars in your name, and yours alone. That way, you won't need my signature any more to write those cheques! You'll sign one for me now and again, if you feel like it."

And since I had no wish to hear her cries of refusal and her disavowals, I very swiftly went back into the flat and slammed the door behind me. Nevertheless, I did have time to catch a cry from the staircase, but one that sounded to me like a cry of surprise rather than protest.

Chapter Six

In Paris, it was one of those late September evenings of magical mildness. The sky still retained its uncompromising blueness – a navy blue, a midnight blue, in fact – that extended just as magnificently from east to west, but with a little more distance than before; and already, and most especial of all, all around its borders the sky was peppered, girdled, deckle-edged with banks of little pink clouds – one of those grey-pinks, a chilly, blotting-paper pink, that the lights of a city discharge into those very low winter skies – and with which the sky would very soon be totally covered. This as yet scarcely descended evening was redolent with the cold of winter, and some gardener or street-sweeper must have lit a fire of dead leaves somewhere not far off, since a pungent and exquisite smell reached us, a smell of decay going back to childhood, and threw in our faces memories of the countryside, all the more poignant if one had never set foot there as a boy.

I had felt a great craving for poetry since my conversations with Coriolan – whom I had met at our favourite café after Laurence had left; to whom I had shown a copy of my agreement with the bank; who now scoured my face with that look full of condescension and affection that I had occasionally seen him give me before, always to my great shame.

"After all," I said, "listen, Laurence can't refuse to sign cheques for me to take my own money out of that bank! That would be incredible!"

"I'd like to think so!"

"But she says she doesn't want any of it!"

"No, she doesn't want it! She doesn't want *you* to have it either! For Laurence, your money is synonymous with blondes, with solo airline tickets and images of you dancing the cha-cha in a casino – without her. Can't you see? She detests that money, and now she can prevent you from having it . . ." He shook his head.

I floundered like an idiot.

"All the same . . . she can't deny me . . ."

"She can deny you the money to buy a packet of cigarettes, if she wants to!" said Coriolan firmly. "Get one thing clear: you may never see a centime of that money. Well, you have to hand it to them! They got you to play straight into their hands!"

I gave an incredulous growl, but I now recalled the joy in my father-in-law's voice . . . And Laurence's gesture in the flat, when she had apparently been scared that I would strike her: if she had been scared, it was because I had good reason to strike her, and I was beginning to see all too clearly what those reasons were. Yet it seemed so unlikely. . .

"She's not going to . . . do you think . . .? really . . .!"

Coriolan shrugged his shoulders without replying, and turned his head away. Then he dispiritedly handed me my papers, patted me on the shoulder, and tilted his chair back, looking spent, mortified . . .

"What time is it?" I asked.

"Don't tell me you're slinking back to the conjugal nest!" He looked shocked.

"But what else do you expect me to do?"

"You really are the limit! Mind you, I knew that. But this time, you amaze me!"

I thought him quaint; was this really the time to leave, just when Coriolan and I could at last have a comfortable, easy life. On the contrary, now was the time to fight, not to run away. I could understand very well what he meant: in my place, he would have drawn the line and made a bid for freedom. And no doubt it was true I should have done something of the sort. But I was a practical man: where would I sleep? In which dreadful suburban hotel, with only one hundred and twenty francs on me, and not even my pyjamas, not even a toothbrush, nothing? When everything was closed and the idea of waking up in some wretched autumnal bedroom struck me as literally appalling. No, I had to go home, to show Laurence that I was aware of her shabby, all but dishonest tricks, and at once lay down the rules of the game so that she should let me use my money. The most difficult thing for me in this affair would be to play the injured party for very long: if there was one mood or sentiment I could never feign for any length of time, it was surely indignation. At any rate, I had never tried it with any success.

But Coriolan had known this for a long time; and he had known too that I would be incapable of provoking the great scene with Laurence that he himself would have had. As usual, everyone knew everything about me in advance, and long before I did. And as usual, my eventual course of behaviour, so predictable and so predicted, prevented me from adopting any other – or rather, spared me from seeking another.

Besides, the truth was, I felt a greater need to cut Laurence down to size than to leave her. And anyway, I was confident I could get round her. If I said to her, "Be nice, give me the money I've earned," I just could not see her replying, "No, I'm keeping it!" I really couldn't. It was unthinkable, between two people who had for so long lived together, slept together, spoken words of love to each other, or listened to them being spoken. Such an attitude, such cynicism were truly impossible. And Laurence set store by her image as a moralist.

On second thoughts, I had no desire whatsoever to talk to her that evening, as things stood, at fever heat. It was beyond my strength. No, I would sleep in my studio and tomorrow morning, as soon as it was dawn, she would be treated to the great performance of charm and virility. So I tiptoed in, noted her absence with relief – her bridge game sometimes carried on till late – and went to bed in my studio. In any case, Laurence did not know what I knew: as far as she was concerned, I, more of a show-off than a fool, wanted to give her what she was taking from me. I had her at a disadvantage. Lulled by the idea of not having to feign either indignation or rage the next day, I fell asleep almost immediately.

I woke up sweltering in the middle of the night. I knew very well why I was being punished: I was being punished for having wanted, if only for ten minutes, to infiltrate, to join the clan of the rich. There had been a moment at the bank when I – so correctly dressed, rehabilitated in the eyes of my father-in-law, regarded with respect by that banker – had felt reassured, at ease, amid that respectability, that comfort and that manifest security. I had felt I was on "their" side. And when that fat banker had explained to me about the interest he extorted from his bank's grasshopper-clients in return for lending them the money belonging to the ants, I had found it almost interesting. I had allowed myself to be seduced by the merchants, by the people I had, after all, been living amongst for almost seven years without any sense of being one of them. I was being punished for my sin in kind, through money – that ugly word, so much uglier than "chart-buster", in which I had believed for that brief moment when I'd had some (or thought I did) and which was actually the same moment in which I had lost it.

At midday I went into Laurence's bedroom. She was sitting up in bed, our bed, munching toast, with a tray on her lap: a rosy, alluring brunette. Maturity would suit her very well. Rather generously proportioned, dark-haired women of her type always blossom with maturity. And for a moment I regretted missing this spectacle (which, after all, nothing prevented me from witnessing). In actual fact, I did not really know what I wanted, hence the precise and limited objective I had set myself. She, at any rate, seemed greatly cheered.

"Hello, darling," she said, stretching out her arms, and I laid my head on her soft, scented shoulder, and so welcoming, so familiar were the feel and the scent of her that I could not believe they were in the service of someone who wished me ill.

It was all nothing but stupidity on her part, vanity and stupidity, plus, of course, the fear of losing me. I frantically sought the proof – proof I hoped for, yearned for – that my wife was truly stupid, even more stupid than I had noted on certain days. And I sat up straight.

"So, not angry any more? How could you have believed that I would let you be snubbed by a bank clerk?"

An expression at once avid, disconcerted, scornful, anxious, and passionate played across her face; she was smiling sadly at something, and I sensed that she was on the verge of feeling sorry for herself.

"I'm just off to the bank," I said, and I sprang to my feet, but stopped dead in mid stride. "Ah, I was forgetting! Before winding up that account, we'll write a cheque together, just one. The only one for which you'll need my signature. Here . . ."

I held out one of the cheques the bank had given me the day before to tide me over. Laurence took it but winced as she read it.

"Three hundred thousand francs! A cheque for three hundred thousand francs! Three hundred thousand new francs?" she repeated, and she stressed the word new as if I were one of those absent-minded old aunts belonging to another age that all good families have, tucked away in the provinces.

"New, yes, yes, of course, new!" I confirmed, smiling, but I could feel myself grinning horribly.

"What for?"

The incredulous and amused tone of her voice forced me to adopt a tone even brighter than hers. And I could see the moment when we were going to succumb to uncontrollable laughter over this wretched cheque.

"A Steinway," I said. "The latest Steinway model. You wouldn't believe the sound it has! It'll be ten years that I'll have dreamt of having one," I added, hoping that this form of the verb would seem convincing to her.

What was it called now? Ah yes, the future perfect! Did it denote "what one had believed, advisedly, in the past, to be the future, an optimistic conditional", or was it not rather "what one had thought possible, even yesterday, and which today turned out to be sweet madness?" The future perfect, yes – but now wasn't the moment to be flirting with the French language. Laurence's face took on a look of pained indulgence, one of her favourite cocktails of assumed expressions.

"Any reason not to have told me?"

I noted in passing her weighty use of the infinitive, more promising, it seemed to me, than the simple past: "Why didn't you tell me?"

My thoughts were flying in all directions without my being able to harness them.

"For exactly that reason – the price!" I explained. "Ah, but you don't have a pen," I said. "Sorry."

I offered her mine with the satisfied air of someone who finally understands the reason for an unexpected delay. Laurence took the pen and reread the cheque for the hundredth time. I stood on one foot by that bed, looking cheerful, and also as if I was in a hurry. I was even rubbing my hands, as though to underline my confidence and haste. And suddenly, in an instant, I knew what hate was. Something rose up inside me, slapped me in the face and made my head swim. Something that, in addition, inspired a dual impulse in me: one to step back to avoid this person before me who was odiously keeping me waiting, the other to step forward, to subdue and crush her on that extravagant bed, to suffocate her. I stood stock still, my heart thumping. This was no frivolous, fleeting feeling, oh no! My arms felt powerless, as though they were hanging down on either side of me, drained of blood, unstrung, useless. At long last I regained possession of them and came to, but it was like the feeling, the sensation you get in your fingers when your hands are frozen; in other words, lacking in solidity, a thoroughly unpleasant, two-way and false contact between skin and flesh.

So, too preoccupied with regaining possession of my senses – an outmoded expression that had until then seemed obscure to me, and which I now finally understood – too preoccupied in short, I scarcely heard Laurence's "No!". I had averted my face when that hatred flooded through me, for fear it might be obvious, and I remained for a moment with my back to Laurence after that "No", with a kind of resignation, the resignation that diplomats must feel when war finally breaks out despite all their efforts: "Into God's hand!" An almost objective resignation and incredulity too: how could she refuse to let me buy, with my own money, an instrument I needed for my work? In retrospect, I was more curious than angry, as though that fit of hatred, so brief and so violent, had drained me of all bitterness.

"No, I don't see what you've got against that Pleyel . . ."

Laurence's voice was offended. She could have been Pleyel's plucky widow confronting two predatory buyers.

"Excuse me," I retorted imperiously. "I don't ask you why you prefer Chanel to Trois-Quartiers. It's just not something that can be put into words."

I was weary of these border incidents and I felt I was being lured into an ambush when she said to me tapping the sheet:

"Vincent, come and sit here!"

I cautiously sat down, facing her, and very briefly I met her gaze – those lovely, staring eyes, silent, dangerous, unseeing like the misaligned headlights of some cars at night.

"Vincent, look at me, please!"

And she took my head in her hands, and drew it close to hers at the risk of being bitten. At the cost of a superhuman effort, I contained myself. She was cheating. This false honesty, this false sincerity, her gaze and mine, so close and in reality so remote from each other – all this bespoke a comedy of such heavy-handedness, of such vulgarity that for the first time I roughly broke free.

"Listen, that's enough! Either I can buy the Steinway with

my royalties, or we say no more about it. And in that case, if that's what you want, I'll write a cheque making the whole amount over to your father."

"I haven't the right, Vincent!" she wailed in a pleading voice. "I haven't the right to let you squander all that money with God knows whom. For you know perfectly well it's not a Steinway that you want to buy, but your mates that you want to help out!"

"So what?"

The fact that she was right did not bother me in the slightest, but that I should have the right to be in the wrong seemed to me obvious, and that she should refuse to subscribe to this, completely abnormal.

"But it does! You'd end up spending it all! You being so guileless, those parasites would take you for everything you have, and at the same time you'd lose your faith in humanity. That, my darling, no, I don't want you to be bitter . . ."

"That's my affair, isn't it?"

"And besides, it was what you wanted, Vincent! Unconsciously, you wanted a bulwark against these people, and you asked for one. You wanted to be protected by responsible people. Think about it! Otherwise, why would you have accepted my father's help?"

"Your father completely hoodwinked me," I said, holding back at the last moment the word "cheated", for I could not decently say that it was cheating me to make me share my wealth. "He didn't explain all the rules to me," I added, "nor for instance, that I wouldn't be able to buy a packet of cigarettes without your permission."

She raised her head with pride.

"Have you ever needed my permission to buy a packet of cigarettes?"

If she was equating my pocket money with my royalties . . . I gave her an eloquent glance that actually made her blush.

"On the other hand, you could draw the interest on your capital every month, which would give you a substantial amount of cash. For that, I'll sign in advance any arrangement you want to make with the bank."

"If I understand correctly, I can spend the fruits of your bankers' usury but not the fruits of my labour? That's perfect!"

"Darling," she said tenderly – and she was almost smiling – "my darling, you're angry, but it's for your sake, Vincent, I swear to you! It's for your sake! You know very well I shan't touch a single franc of your money. I'm keeping it for you, that's all. That's what you want, in fact, without realizing it." (This little Freudian touch was obviously the final stone in the edifice created to shelter her good conscience: an unshakeable structure that, in the interval between the previous evening and that morning, she had erected, with the invincible strength of stupidity and dishonesty, combined with her very real possessiveness.)

I was not equipped to contend with such simple, strong sentiments and desires, nor with the weapons she used, against which there was no defence.

"But I'm only thinking of you, Vincent! Imagine if something happened to me, my darling . . ."

"Don't conjure up catastrophes," I said in a final burst of irony, just before something stuck in my throat and forced me to leave the room, almost backing my way out, red-faced and stumbling, before the panic-stricken gaze of my loving wife. I felt a kind of nervous nausea such as I had not suffered for years, not since my adolescence in fact, and which at the time I believed corresponded to psychological problems to be expected at that age, problems of which I had thought I was free for ever.

I returned to my studio, my refuge, locked the door and lay down on my bed. She had certainly got the better of me! For seven years she had cared nothing about humiliating me, she had simply wanted me to be there, even if angry and hiding my anger. She had always dreamed of controlling me, and of letting me know that she controlled me. It deeply rankled her to support me, and she must have thought that I stayed with her solely for that reason, that I was like her conceited swine of a father – the difference being, I was unable to hurt her, as her poor mother had been hurt all her life. Laurence must have witnessed this sorry state of affairs throughout her adolescence and vowed to spare herself that: the arrogance and boorishness of an unfaithful husband. That was the reason she had married me: because she thought me weak, and imagined she could prevent me from deceiving her. She had always been the owner and I her property. She had never loved me, she had owned me. As for those failures that had put me to shame, she had only consoled me because they suited her. She did not want a great virtuoso, she would even have done her utmost to prevent me from becoming one, had I ever had the makings of one.

And what distressed me, what hurt the sentimental cynic in me – this being my true nature – was the memory of those moments when I had in fact loved her a little, when I had taken pleasure in seeing her happy and believing her to be happy, moments that had never existed. Far from it. She had duped me, she had taken advantage of me, she had lived off me, sponging on my good humour, my robust temperament, my natural cheerfulness. She had observed them and exploited them in an atmosphere of perpetual tension that was never relaxed. She had said to me a thousand times, "I love you," for the sole reason that love was for her an extra, a bonus, whereas I said it to her because I believed it, because I wanted to believe it.

And yet I had been bored with her, desperately bored. I had tolerated her dreadful friends, her boastfulness, her callousness, her stupidity, her snobbishness, with culpable forbearance. Or rather a forbearance inspired by guilt, the guilt I sometimes felt at the idea of her supporting me as she did, a guilt I should never have felt, however, had she been generous with a touch of grace and naturalness; in short, had she loved me for myself.

But now I was a captive, I had not the strength to start again from scratch, with no job, no friends, no money and above all no recent experience of being poor. She had taken the best years of my life, as though *I* were a woman and she a man. And whatever happened in bed in no way altered that. She had only really loved me for her own sake. She did not know me, she was not interested in me; to realize the truth of this, I had only to recall how vigorously she would correct in me anything that did not suit her. A kind of dry sob escaped me, and the thought came to me that Laurence was making me cry for the first time; but cry with shame for she had duped me.

I recalled that evening when we were lying in bed, the second time she had slept in it, in that dismal hotel room where I was living at the time, in avenue Coty, and where we had decided to get married. She had not asked me if I loved her, she had told me that she loved me, that she wanted to live with me, and that I would be happy with her. I had certainly raised the objection that I was not sure I loved her; it was of no importance, she had replied, I would one day. She had even added, unsubtly but flatteringly, "As long as you keep pretending as well as you do, my darling!" It was after we had made love, and I had believed her; I had believed myself. And here I was, seven years later, trapped, egotistic, incompetent and cynical, and now ridiculous. "Bravo," I said to myself, "bravo! For once you care to draw up a balance sheet, to take stock of the situation, and there's no denying how brilliant it looks! Bravo, my dear Vincent!" But what frightened me, in retrospect, even more than the future, was the idea of having been able to live for seven years, to have slept for seven years, with someone who had never loved me, who had never felt for me anything but passion at its worst – if that is what one could call that single-minded cupidity of hers.

I had returned to my studio, now my temporary hideout, prepared to go back to sleep. But it was only one o'clock in the afternoon. I had suffered more reversals, more pyschological or emotional traumas, within the space of an hour than during the entire week. I had to get out, but where to go? For a moment I hesitated to take the car. Instead of feeling relieved of the duties of a husband, I felt deprived of the rights of a gigolo. Since Laurence had not loved me and did not love me (at least, no more than she might have loved any male who was vigorous, presentable and amenable), I was no longer entitled to anything. So what was I going to do with myself? "Pretend! You're going to pretend!" a shrill and prudent voice prompted me. "Pretend not to have understood a thing, pretend to laugh, pretend to forget! Pretend! Always pretend!"

I had some business matters to deal with. I had to go and see Not-a-sou, to consider with him ways of escaping the clutches of my family-in-law. In my rebellion, I put on my new suit again – the one Laurence hated, the one that was badly made, of bad material, and made me look bad – and then went out. I passed Odile on the staircase as she was coming in, and she gave me a big smile. I returned it with a wink, wondering what version of the story Laurence would dish out to her, what version her vanity or her moralism would dictate.

So I went off to Not-a-sou by myself, since Coriolan stood in for a bookmaker every Thursday. I was kept waiting at Delta Blues, and with the rain coming down on the chestnut trees, I found it to be true that, as the saying goes, time passes and no two days are the same. When I went into Not-a-sou's office, he seemed very surly.

"So you're here!" he grumbled. "Well, you'll have to forgive me, I received the letter from your bank this morning, but I haven't had time yet to put all your statements together."

"What letter?"

"The one you sent me yesterday. Congratulations, eh, so you fire off powers of attorney and send out demands for settlement, just like a debt collector! To read your letter, I could have taken myself for a crook! Anyhow, your father-in-law is sending over some expert tomorrow to go through my books . . ."

"I've nothing to do with it," I confessed piteously.

"Well, I have to admit, you've been conned in no uncertain manner, and that's the truth of it! You're not going to get a single franc out of that 'Showers' of yours, old man! Not a kopeck!"

"That's not exactly why . . ."

"Well, I'm going to tell you something," continued Not-a-sou, absolutely beside himself. "You know what I think? So much the better! Because I tell you, being a composer, and hits, and all that, and success, it's not for amateurs, you understand! A hit isn't something you come across by chance, one fine morning, just strumming on a piano!"

"Yet that's how I came across 'Showers'."

"Just as I thought! Just as I thought! Only now I know what really happened! Believe it or not, I had dinner with your friend Bonnat, the film director. He told me the whole story!"

"What did he tell you?"

"Well, now, that the idea for the tune – doh, te, lah, fah, or whatever it was – came from a friend of his, and that you had arranged it, badly as it happens, but immediately claimed the copyright; and that he had to get it rerecorded afterwards, by a third party, but to your advantage . . . Well done, old boy, well done!"

Stunned by this, I cut him short.

"Seriously, Bonnat told you that?"

"Yes, yes, and," he further added with vehemence, "I believed him. I'm sorry, but between a man like Bonnat, who enjoys the work he does, and a fellow like you, whose only talent is for having his bank, or his wife's bank, send out demands for payment, I don't have much hesitation . . . Mind you, your wife has come out of it magnificently. It's true, it must be no joke being married to a gigolo, that too has to be admitted!"

"Oh dear," I thought wearily, "I'm going to have to hit him . . ." And mentally I looked for a way to avoid it. Only my nerves, working faster than my head, had seized the initiative and already my fist was missing Not-a-sou's chin, but catching him on the cheek. He reeled back three paces, shouting: "Watch it, hey, watch it, old boy! Watch it!" A threat immediately invalidated since he fell heavily to the ground, his thick-pile carpet at last turning out to have some use.

"You'll pay for that!" he yelled from the floor, pointing his index finger at me. "You'll pay for that!"

I in turn pointed my index finger at him, but I was laughing:

"I really don't see what I could pay for right now, eh?" I said, mimicking him.

As I left, I caught the looks of delight, indeed of gratitude for this knock-out, on his employees' faces. I shut the door of that office, where, heaven knows why, I had imagined myself turning up from time to time to discuss my affairs, my plans, like any ordinary man . . . An office! I had almost had an office! The very idea! My heart still pounding after that little fit of temper, I went and sat down on a café terrace and ordered myself a whisky, like a big boy. I most certainly had to remember to thump Xavier Bonnat if I ever ran into him again . . . But I did not trust myself on that score either. My grudges were as short-lived as my anger and already I felt sorry for poor old Not-a-sou, harassed by my father-in-law's bailiffs; already I felt almost sorry, too, for Xavier Bonnat, the failure of whose financial plans had led him to tell such pathetic lies. All the same . . . it was one hard knock after another, and my prospects were becoming gloomier by the minute. I raised my hand to call the waiter. My second whisky was not so good as the third, which was not so good as the fourth, etc. etc. In short, by four in the afternoon I was dead drunk on the terrace of Fouquet's, and very happy to be so. I had to be careful not to go home; I always became very big-hearted, very affectionate when I drank, and I could very well imagine myself, brimming over with love and forgetfulness, in Laurence's arms. (And something told me that I should not do this.) I could go and see Coriolan in his bar, but I had never set foot in the place before, which was a sure sign he did not really want me to. Otherwise . . . well, otherwise, to be honest, I had nowhere to go. I had no other male friends – Laurence had got rid of them – and of course, no female friends any more, either. As an only child, with both parents dead, nor did I have any family to fall back on. True, that left me with a few loving mistresses – often friends of Laurence – but those affairs went back two or three years, Laurence having also deprived me of the taste for amorous intrigue. That still left me with gambling, but no one would lend me a decent amount in exchange for a dud cheque. I had enough for my drinks, full stop. So I paid for my whiskies, leaving a generous tip, and to my great surprise, in the bottom of my pocket I found one thousand five hundred francs – Coriolan's envelope – left over from my one day as a rich man. That's what I had been for one whole day – a rich man! Not everyone was so lucky, although I had not had much time to enjoy it. I cautiously got to my feet, and noted that my system was still carrying its alcohol well. I could walk in a straight line, although with my head slightly tilted to one side, like a real Al Capone. All I needed was the hat. I hastened to buy one in a shop, which left me with only seven hundred francs, and came back to my table. There was no question of my going home with those seven hundred francs; I was sure that Laurence or her father would grab them from my pocket the minute I arrived. "No, they won't get the better of me this time," I mumbled, "that's too easy! Oh, no, not this time!" I looked round for my car, in vain, but eventually my eyes lit upon an utterly charming, so-called "lady of pleasure". Being a little tipsy, I told her how much money I had before she quoted her price.

"I've seven hundred francs," I declared as I accosted her.

"That's lucky," she said quite kindly, "I haven't." And I followed her.

I spent two very pleasant hours with Jeannine. Resigned to Laurence's prohibitions, I had forgotten the joys of physical licence and I rediscovered them with delight, even took some comfort from them: for if Laurence had not allowed me certain liberties, this meant I had not revealed to her the pleasures of them either. Encouraged by the alcohol, I was full of tenderness towards my companion, a tenderness she tolerated with good humour. I was even sorry to leave her, never having been disheartened by making love, unlike some. That dark little room, with its brown carpet, its green curtains patterned with graceful, multicoloured flowers, its screen of the same quality, seemed to me, if not more elegant, at least more homely than boulevard Raspail. But I really had to go, to leave Jeannine, to find my car again, which took me an infinite amount of time.

Coriolan left his café at six; I went and parked outside it a little before that. He came out exactly on time, and I revved up the engine of my car. I had pulled my hat down over my eyes, and he raised his eyebrows as he bent down at the door.

"What are you playing at?"

"Al Capone!" I said. "But you must see me in action!"

"You're completely drunk!" he declared, nevertheless settling into the dead man's seat.

I was not really drunk any more. So I went back with him to the Lion de Belfort and drank what was necessary to return me to that blessed state. Coriolan's laughter was forced; he had some bad news to tell me, he said, but he had bowed to my refusal to listen, and joked with me. For Coriolan was a real friend! I now had Jeannine as a friend too, as well as him, which warmed my heart. And then there was Serge, who owned the café, a real pal; and my father-in-law's butler, good old Thomas, now, alas, dead! The memory of the funeral ode that his former employer had concocted came into my mind, and I enthusiastically related it to Coriolan. I then recounted to him the few verbal swipes I had so cleverly taken against my father-in-law before allowing myself to be ruined by him. And I scored another big success, this time with the whole café – in other words, four not very discriminating onlookers. So I had completely cheered up by dinner time and felt little inclined to go home. Or rather, to Laurence's.

"You know," I confided to Coriolan, "she doesn't love me, she's never loved me!"

One of Coriolan's charms was that he never stooped to saying, "I told you so!" – although truly, in my case, there had been more than one occasion on which he might have done so.

"She values you," he said. "That's something different."

"Do you remember," I began, "when . . ."

Very much *à propos*, I recalled an offer I had been made, three years earlier, of a job with a music journal, an offer I'd had to turn down. It certainly would not have made me rich, but it was a way of earning a living.

"Well," I explained to Coriolan, to refresh his memory, "Laurence did her utmost to make it impossible."

"What did she do?" asked Coriolan, increasingly willing, helped on by the alcohol, to listen to anything.

"Her appendicitis!" I said. "Her appendicitis! Just as I was about to accept that job, she had appendicitis, followed by peritonitis. I even had to sleep at the clinic. As soon as the job was taken by someone else, hup, she miraculously recovered."

I had been very scared then that Laurence might die. I had been horribly upset in anticipation. I could remember having imagined her death without the slightest sense of relief, and yet . . .! At that time she did not want me to work and now she blamed me for not having done so. Really, it was incredible!

"What if I got a job?" I asked the assembled company.

Coriolan examined his hands studiously, as though his mind was on something else. I shook him.

"Well?"

"Uh, right now, there's a lot of unemployment, you know," he mumbled. "You don't stand much chance of finding anything without contacts."

"I can always try!"

It wasn't such a stupid idea: after all, what objection could Laurence raise if I got up in the morning and spent the day working? What would Laurence do from morning till evening without her big toy? On the other hand, the big toy named Vincent had always had trouble getting up at dawn, a detail not to be overlooked.

"Listen," said Coriolan, "the bad news I told you about:

I went to see Not-a-sou with the agent's contract you drew up for me. He laughed in my face! Twenty-five per cent is illegal. Apparently, it could even carry a prison sentence. I can't even ask him for ten per cent, now that he has the original contract in his hands. Mind you, he swore not to bring proceedings against me."

"Well, that's something. By the way, you know, I roughed him up today – Not-a-sou, that is!"

The other customers, who had wandered off for a moment during our private conversation, at these words suddenly reappeared. I described to them with a wealth of more or less accurate detail my fight with the unfortunate director of Delta Blues. I concluded sentimentally:

"And afterwards, I went to see Jeannine, for a beautiful end to the day."

I had forgotten how diverting life on the streets of Paris could be. I had deprived myself of it for seven years because Laurence was hurt by my absences, because Laurence was hurt if she did not have her big toy. (In my drunkenness this expression struck me as hilarious.) On the other hand, I could not care less about Coriolan's lack of success: in the position we were now in, neither twenty-five per cent nor ten per cent of my earnings was going to secure us freedom or wealth.

"Let's drink to that!" I declared. "Gentlemen, the drinks are on me."

It was only then that I remembered I had given all my money to Jeannine. Life in the outside world was as ruinously expensive as it was fun. Thank God for Coriolan: of the money from yesterday, he had kept a hundred thousand francs in cash, just in case. I rubbed my hands.

"So, we still have nearly one hundred thousand francs left."

"We do indeed!"

"Well, we're going to make the most of them, old man. Tomorrow, we go to Evry!"

"Longchamp!" said Coriolan sternly. "On Mondays, it's Longchamp." His eyes were shining.

"What are you gentlemen drinking?" I repeated – and we abandoned our brief careers as composer and agent.

I came home drunk. In the silence and darkness of the flat, I made my way to my studio without running into too many obstacles, apart from an enormous, brand-new Steinway, waiting for me there. I was amazed, then sickened. Despite the beauty of the instrument, I did not allow myself to play it; I restricted myself to stroking the keys. Tomorrow morning, I would enter the marital bedroom without knocking, and explain to Laurence the difference between a longed-for piano and a piano conceded.

Which is what I tried to do as soon as I woke up, but she had already gone. Back in my studio, I spent two hours trying out the piano. Whatever music I played sounded magnificent, delicate, different, unfurling and flowing from my fingers; whether it was Beethoven, which I jazzed up, or Fats Waller, which I played lingeringly, it was all fresh, all dazzling. After two hours I was a man again, a young man mad about music, the good old Vincent I used to be; I was at last at one with myself. Worse, I was happy, albeit against my will.

This was actually the first time ever that I found happiness or the pleasure of life inopportune. In the last seven years I had lost the taste for the unexpected and no doubt acquired a taste for the leash. I had lost certain qualities I was sure I had once possessed: cheerfulness, confidence, a readiness to enjoy life – three instinctive qualities that had gradually been replaced by others, which were cultivated: reserve, irony and indifference. These three virtues would be of use to me in frustrating Laurence's plans. She would be armed with her natural assets: vanity, selfishness and dishonesty, all three magnified tenfold by her terrible, violent desire for possession, a desire that unfortunately did not exist in me. I had only one desire: to escape her! However, I did not have the means . . . In any case, it would be an unequal struggle: because I would take as much displeasure in using my bad weapons as in noting the weakness, the uselessness of my good ones; and because a combat becomes unequal from the moment one of the combatants is wounded by his own hand.

This dark train of thought was suddenly interrupted by a merry rattle from the next room. It was Odile, at the electric typewriter, energetically starting on her mail, or rather my mail. I went in.

"Hello!" I said gaily. "You know, my dear Odile, you owe me no further respect, nor any more typing? I have consigned all my possessions and all my rights to Laurence. She's the one with whom you will administer my ex-fortune."

"Sorry? What do you mean?"

Odile had a very precise, ringing voice, one that was hard, too, on a man who had been drinking the day before. I raised my hand to my forehead while she exclaimed:

"It's not true? You're joking!"

She seemed stunned. I solemnly replied:

"It's the least I could do, Odile, considering . . . Think what I must have cost my wife these past seven years."

Odile blushed. Then adopting an authoritative, business-like voice I did not recognize as hers, she brandished her pencil at me.

"On a personal level, I don't know what you owe Laurence, but on a purely financial level, if you really have earned one million dollars, as she told me . . ."

"It's true," I sorrowfully acknowledged. "Yes, indeed, one million dollars."

"Well, that means you'll be paying her back about seventy thousand francs a month. But you've never cost Laurence that much."

"Pardon?"

For the first time ever, she seemed full of confidence and wisdom. "Well, let's think about it: let's say it's six francs to the dollar. So your one million dollars gives you six million new francs. If I divide that amount by seven for your seven years, that comes to more than eight hundred and fifty thousand francs per year; divided by twelve, is roughly seventy thousand francs a month! Now, I don't believe you've ever spent that amount, or even that Laurence spent it on your monthly keep. Far from it."

I burst out laughing. It was the last thing I had expected.

"I hadn't thought about it, but it's true. How much do you think I could have cost Laurence each month? Roughly, of course."

"Much less. Really, much less!" she exlaimed earnestly. "Would you like us to work it out?"

And she was obligingly reaching for her calculator when I stopped her with a wave of my hand.

"No, I was only joking. Honest, it was a joke! In any case, I'm delighted, Odile! It proves that in addition to a happy marriage, Laurence will have also made a profit! So much the better! For once, I represent a good investment . . ."

Odile bowed her head, now torn, it seemed, between embarrassment and fear.

"I told you that, Vincent, out of friendship . . . for . . ."

"It was very kind of you, my dear Odile, and I'm truly grateful. Of course, I shan't say a word to Laurence. If it comes to the worst, I shall tell her it was I who worked out those figures."

There was a pause. Then she made up her mind to say something:

"You know, Vincent, I'd like to tell you . . . Laurence is like any other woman; she would rather have a present that you'd chosen for her, than an account simply opened in a bank. All women are the same, about that, I can assure you!"

"Not my wife! Not Laurence! I married a rare creature," I added, hoping, altruistically, that the majority of wives who provide for their husbands cherish and support their penniless menfolk without keeping them tied up at home.

"Why haven't you had any children?" asked Odile just as I was going through the door.

I did not answer. Even the day before, I would have hesitated to say to her, "We're thinking about it." But we were not thinking about it. We had never thought about it. Or rather, Laurence must have thought about it by herself and decided that she did not want another toy, not even a very little one; she was happy with the big one. She must have been afraid that the little toy might be enchanting and that the big toy might then take his eyes off her own lovely self for an instant. And besides, no doubt in her family, it was not done to have children by paupers; there was a limit to everything, even to an unsuitable marriage. In certain cases, children went by the board.

Odile's calculations – petty, but surely accurate – still preyed on my mind. In marrying me, Laurence had got herself a good deal – although a risky one, on the face of it. Thinking about it logically, it was true that I ate little, that I was quite frugal, slim, easy to dress. Naturally, there had been some expensive purchases, such as the car, the gold cuff-links (four pairs, which must have added up to a tidy sum); there had even been the camera, old now but still functional. That was all . . . and it was not my pocket money that was going to tip the balance in her favour! "How dreadful!" I said to myself. "How dreadful these calculations are, even in jest! How tasteless! And what's the good . . ."

Even if it was her fault, even if Laurence was responsible for all that, I refused to wallow in such small-mindedness. It was time I had done with this apartment that I found too small, with this bedroom where her love had so often suffocated me, with all these rooms in which I had lived surrounded by faces as closed to me as the shutters were kept closed. Ah, when all was said and done, I had been alone here for seven years. Alone, so alone! With no shared laughter, not a thought in common. Together, we had uttered only cries of sexual pleasure, and even then, never at the same time . . . I banged my head against a wall to punish myself, to stop that sour and squalid voice within me that spoke and thought in my stead, a voice unbearable to listen to, but irrepressible.

When I woke up a little later, I realized simultaneously that it was midday and that I had forgotten to include my watch in that aforementioned inventory (and – what an ungrateful wretch! – a watch from Place Vendôme, at that). So, it was midday, I would go to the races at about three, I would be home at about seven. Once again, it was such-and-such a time. The hours had returned, whereas for seven years they had been lost. That long stretch of time shared with Laurence, time that could not be computed in hours – dead time – was back on the clock, and my new-found interest in the position of the two hands seemed to me a sign of resurrection. And the time when life had slipped by for seven years, like a dream, seemed something of a nightmare.

"Showers" was playing, once again, on Odile's radio, but I remembered that it did not belong to me any more, it was a tune of Xavier Bonnat's that I had supposedly misappropriated and spoiled after my own fashion . . . Oh yes, I would certainly take a swing at dear Xavier the next time I saw him. This prospect cheered me, until I realized that it implied my return to Laurence. After all, I could not stay on after what she had done! Unfortunately, "after all" had never carried much weight in my thinking, or had much influence on my actions. I had "after all" passed my *baccalauréat*, I had "after all" been accepted at the Conservatoire, Laurence had "after all" married me. But all these "after alls" derived from other people, from teachers or women, and often seemed like "in spite ofs". "In spite of Vincent!" On the other hand, it was I, after all, who put on the brown Al Capone suit and telephoned Coriolan. An hour later, we were in the car, on the way to Longchamp, not without having dropped in at my bank, where we had withdrawn some of my capital and shared it between us. We felt not a little proud, never having had such a large amount to play on the horses.

The weather was fine and Longchamp as wonderful as it had always been. In seven years, I had been able to go there only three times: the first time with Laurence, who liked the social trappings of the Arc de Triomphe, but my immediate disappearance for three hours had set her against racing; the second time, when, having been snatched from death, she'd had to stay in bed after her appendicitis; and the third, when she had gone to Brittany for the funeral of her father's father (who could not bear even the mention of my name). In short, over a period of seven years, I would have been to the races only four times, thanks to this woman and in spite of her: (a) thanks to her snobbishness; (b) thanks to her illness; (c) thanks to one of her relatives; and (d) today, thanks to her duplicity. But I had never needed anyone to send me rushing off to wonderful, delightful Longchamp.

Naturally, I ran into a number of racegoing friends or acquaintances, who greeted me as though I had left only yesterday. Whilst the hours pass very quickly at Longchamp, the years do not penetrate; here, a person ages three years during a race, but then gains not a wrinkle for the next one and a half decades. Anyway, the wrinkles acquired here are lines of excitement, nervousness, disappointment, enthusiasm and exultation, but these are not serious wrinkles – at any rate, not the devastating, dishonourable wrinkles of boredom. Coriolan explained this by the unreal nature that money assumes on these other planets – for such are racing tracks – where the pursuit of it, possession of it, depends entirely on capricious quadrupeds; where a hundred francs on the last race is ten times more exciting than a thousand on the first. Where you chat affably to professional tipsters whose tips have already lost you a fortune, but you smile to them; you might even go along with them in the next race, something difficult to imagine happening at the Stock Exchange. Where, after all, my father-in-law, had he been a racegoer, would have found himself rubbing shoulders with his butlers, and got no respect from them, would even have attracted downright scorn, if he had been fool enough to put a lot of money, in their presence, on some old hack.

In short, I found myself once again surrounded by free spirits, happy-go-lucky and affectionate people. I fancied that the heavens were opening and angels playing for me on their trumpets the hymn to life – life rediscovered, real life, normal life. To my great astonishment and to the amazement of Coriolan, who was watching me at that moment, I suddenly had tears in my eyes, genuine salt tears. And I even had to wipe my face on my sleeve, close one eye and rail against the wretched dust that had got into the other, so as not to cover myself with shame. But I was a little slow off the mark, and throughout the meeting Coriolan kept giving me sideways glances – worried, even fearful glances – as one might eye a restive horse.

After this reunion, we went upstairs to the boxes, where we knew a few of the owners, who greeted us with open arms. We stayed there for three or four races, to the – discreet – surprise of our hosts, the state of our finances generally barring us from more than half an hour on that floor, from which the fifty-franc betting counters were excluded. This time, thanks to Not-a-sou's first and last cheque, we were able to make a splash. After the fourth race, I went downstairs, enthusiastic and excited, and met a few people. And in the enclosure, I lost my heart to a light chestnut mare called Sanseverina. Why she took my fancy, I still don't know. She was down at 42 to 1 – a bad sign, but all the same I made up my mind, in a moment of madness, to place everything I had on her. I had lost, won, lost, and I now just had my head above water after two hours' work, which was vexing, more vexing in some ways than losing. As for Coriolan, I had absolutely no idea how he stood. We never told each other what we were betting – a line of conduct that we thought brilliant when the other lost, and idiotic when he won, but which spared us the reproaches and remorse, or even regrets, that joint betting always leads to in the end.

That day, however, when I passed Coriolan on my way back from the betting counters, he asked me what I had bet, and to my further surprise did not burst into ironic laughter when I confessed I had put the whole lot on Sanseverina. He confined himself to shrugging his shoulders, and arranged to meet me by the nearest stands. I quietly waited there for him, while the crowd gathered and the horses lined up for the start. It was a 2100-metre course and no sooner were they off than the commentator put Sanseverina in the lead. Logically, my hopes should have died then; an outsider leading from the start had absolutely no chance of crossing the line in the same position. Yet I waited like everyone else, straining my neck towards the bend out of which the front-runners would appear. And soon, very soon, I heard a kind of drone, then a rumble as the horses, like some great hornet, come to the last turn, over there. It was a very particular kind of rumble, which increased as the crowd joined in with its voice and clamour, the crowd that was gathered in the public enclosure by the finishing post. A uniform, indistinct rumble, which swelled without fragmenting, up to a certain point, always at exactly the same level, two hundred metres from the line, when suddenly it would seem that the crowd had lost its voice and the horses no longer advanced. Just after that, the clamour and the rumble became immense but distinct, the thousands of voices shouting the names of horses no longer drowning that frenetic thundering of dozens of hoofs on the ground, that age-old sound, that wild horde, that terrifying and barbaric charge that must awaken in us memories of the distant past. For it was impossible to tell, at that moment, if the crowd was yelling with terror or excitement. I drew a cigarette from my pocket as the announcement came that Sanseverina was still among the front-runners, but joined now by Patchouli (the favourite). I sadly lit my cigarette, then dropped it when the commentator added: "Sanseverina seems to be holding off Patchouli's challenge!" I closed my eyes for a moment, allowing myself a profane prayer, and before I even saw them, I heard those in the lead coming towards us, making that furious din, marked by the clinking of bits and stirrups, the squeak of leather, and the muttered oaths of the jockeys bent over their saddles. Then I opened my eyes and I saw the multicoloured welter of caps, floating like a standard over the straining bodies of the horses, glistening with sweat, sinewy and so naked. And while the pack passed in front of me with that sound of ripping fabric, and while the clamour of the crowd exploded and died away at the finish, someone began to shout over the loudspeaker: "Sanseverina is the winner! Sanseverina held out to the finish! First, Sanseverina! A photo-finish for Patchouli and Noumea!" And while my cigarette burnt a hole in one of my Italian mocassins, I experienced one of the most glorious moments of my life, a pleasure so violent and so pure, so complete that it became honourable. I had won! I had won against the whole world! I had won against my father-in-law, a banker, a producer, my director, my wife and the PMU!* I was a winner! And while my disappointed neighbours threw their tickets to the ground, I leapt into the arms of Coriolan, who had just come up, shouting: "I won!"

"We won!" he crowed, slapping me on the back, and surprise made my pleasure twice as great.

"You bet on her too?"

"I did," he said. "I even went and put five hundred francs on her!"

"And I bet two thousand! But how come you backed Sanseverina?"

We returned to the betting counters, laughing, surrounded by unlucky punters who watched us with that envious scorn that serious racegoers have for those who win on outsiders.

"But I told you I was backing her?"

Coriolan laughed cheerfully.

"Today, I followed your lead in every race, old man! I told myself that with everything that had already happened to you, you couldn't lose on the horses as well."

And he burst out laughing, his laughter fearless if not tactful. But I did not give a damn for tact. Sanseverina had come in at 37 to 1. I had therefore won seventy-four thousand francs, something that had never happened to me before, with good reason! I offered to buy drinks all round, for the whole crowd, who now suddenly revived.

We returned to Paris drunk with pride. At a red light, Coriolan turned to me:

"For a fellow who had seven million francs filched from his bank account yesterday, you look fairly pleased!"

But there was no one better able than he to understand how winning seventy thousand francs at the races could be more exhilarating than having seven million in a bank.

**Paris mutuel urbain*=French state betting system.

Chapter Seven

So I returned home triumphant, not without having entrusted my winnings to Coriolan. A bitter memory now discouraged me from leaving my belongings lying around at Laurence's. Naturally, the money from the races was bound to seem unsavoury to her, but I had learnt to my cost how consuming her distaste could be.

For two days now I had been saying "at Laurence's" with as much ease as I had once had difficulty in saying "at our place", after being married for six months – five of them spent on honeymoon, and one in a hotel. For ours had been a long honeymoon, a very long honeymoon – in Italy, of course. Better still, in Capri. A Capri with which Laurence had not, until then, wanted to acquaint herself. "This will seem silly to you," she had told me, "but the more I was told how nice it was, the more determined I was only to go there with someone I really loved. Do you think me absurd?"

"No, of course not," I had replied with a smile. "On the contrary . . ."

I had never been to Capri either, for completely different reasons. But I must confess that at the time I found the whole thing a joke – the idea of me, Vincent, newly married, spending his honeymoon with his biddable, beautiful, wealthy bride visiting the Blue Grotto, the Fariglioni, Axel Munthe's villa, etc. etc. – and why not? Why not probe the commonplace and visit picture-postcard locations? It was just as much fun as systematically rejecting them – just as much fun and less snobbish. Especially as my only trip to Italy had been with a group of Italian quasi-artists and self-styled ecologists whom I had encountered in Paris, and who had turned out, in the course of our travels, to be real hoodlums. I had even had to put up a fight to get away from them after they had ransacked a service station – all of this conducted on clapped-out motorbikes in the pouring rain! For it had rained incessantly in Italy that year. Consequently, I had marvelled during that honeymoon at the sun's graciousness and obligingness towards sentimental, privileged tourists.

So we had walked hand in hand in the little streets of Capri. Laurence had bought what was probably the only worthwhile piece of jewellery in the piazzetta: a black pearl in a charming, antique platinum setting. And for nothing: Laurence, like all her family, adored getting a bargain. And, following their example, she would readily have bought a Van Gogh for one hundred francs from a blind dealer without telling him of its value, still less sharing it with him ... Perhaps I had only survived all that time because I was not expensive. Besides, I was an exceptional case, I had completely refunded my expenses. Legally, I could leave. But then, what about my alimony? "Your alimony?" people will say. "What alimony? With such a lovely wife, and so devoted? What do you mean, alimony?" How could anyone be so boorish? And yet, and yet, it was, almost as much as my worry about poverty, the thought of having been robbed that prevented me from leaving. Robbed, not financially or physically, robbed in another respect ...

When I recalled that honeymoon and Laurence's enthusiasm, her modesty, in those days! She was so anxious to please me! She spent her whole time fretting about her foolishness and its disastrous effects on the love I might have for her. And of course, I, who already detested power struggles, who despised men guilty of compliancy towards their hysterical wives, did everything I could to reassure her, those few verbal mannerisms of hers, those few unpleasant responses she had, seeming to me to owe more to her background than to her character, poor fool that I was! I had credited her with twenty different qualities, but, even assuming she had them, I had not imagined that she might lack that manner of deploying them which alone would make them tolerable; a manner that no education, however sophisticated, can teach. Laurence, for instance, was intelligent but without wit, lavish without generosity, beautiful without charm, staunch without goodness, excited without zest, envious without desire. She was disparaging without hatred, arrogant without pride, familiar without warmth, and sensitive without vulnerability. She was childish but unchildlike, plaintive without abandon, well dressed without elegance, and furious without anger. She was direct without loyalty, timorous without fear, in short passionate without love. I picked up a pencil and my famous music notebook, which were in my car, and I carefully wrote down what I would call the Litany of St Laurence, and I repeated to myself all these formulas, sometimes altering them, changing the order of one adjective or another, each time finding them more accurate, more acute. Carried away by my prose, assuaged if not revenged, I got out of the car at boulevard Raspail, slamming the door with the slow, expansive gesture of those peaceable administrators of justice – all of a sudden, rightly angry – who appear in American TV series. I suddenly remembered a serial in which a team of astronauts aboard a flying-saucer were travelling in space in the year 3000, cruising amid stars unknown to any living being (and amid sentiments of universal triteness). Now, one fine evening, Laurence had wanted to change over to another series at the same time. Why had I let her deprive me of my spaceship and my heroes with pointed ears? How could I have agreed to it? By what despotism had she imposed on me instead the antics of some bronzed creeps in Los Angeles? I was unable to remember. All I knew was that for nearly a month Coriolan had told me what happened in subsequent episodes of my serial, until he could not bear to watch it any more. Why had Laurence not bought herself another television? Why had I not bought one myself? I knew the answer to that: it would have put too much of a strain on my pocket money. And how and why had I been able to do without a dog, when I loved dogs? And why did I not have more friends whom I could invite home for a drink? And more to the point, why had it become so little my home that I had not been able to invite anyone there, in the days when I still had some friends? And why did I have to invent complicated excuses simply to go out for a walk? And why was the fact that I went out described as leaving her? What was the reason for my not having told her that her friends were arrogant, inane, conventional, that two centuries ago they would have justified the use of the guillotine? How could I have so far ignored my own desires and regarded her sudden changes of mood as so many decrees that could not be circumvented, so many quasi-meteorological climates? Why, how, thanks to whom, in spite of what? Even now, when I was more selfish, more cowardly and more indifferent to my fate, I found it hard to understand. At the beginning ... at the beginning, how could I have let my life, my time, be controlled in that way, without any rebellion, without the slightest conflict? Had she proceeded slowly, deliberately, like a real tactician ... or else, a tyrant by nature, a born bully, had she simply allowed herself to be guided by her instincts? And done so without my calling out: "Stop!" Or rather, in view of my character, without my once muttering on the stairs (at least as a ploy): "I think I've had enough of this. Good-bye, darling."

I could not actually remember – and it was this more than anything that frightened me – a single proper argument, a single big row, a single towering rage, and therefore a single occasion when we had spent three days apart! I could not remember a single one of those bursts of hatred that mark the life of a happy couple. She had tentatively wept, I had tentatively wiped away her tears – at first, it seemed to me, every three months; then, latterly, not at all. With Laurence, there were neither tears nor storms, even though she was as turbulent as a lake, dull as a lake, and now, like a lake, dangerous. Where was my litany? "Dangerous without hazard and restless without fervour ..." Yes, they were two good formulas and I added them to the others. I closed my notebook and automatically stuffed it in my pocket: an old reflex told me on no account to leave it lying around. But actually, yes. It was imperative that Laurence should find it, read it or let me read it to her. The crafty, disobedient child in me ought to give way to a man, a real man. I sniggered: since I had formulated and written down my disrespectful litany, my thoughts were casting themselves in the form of sentences. A curt and irritated self within me no longer exclaimed: "My God, what a bitch she is! What a bitch!" But instead, the same acid voice as the day before told me: "Darling Laurence is a pernicious animal. It's high time you got away from her, and the sooner, the better, my dear fellow." Yes, indeed . . . "my dear fellow"! I was addressing myself as "my dear fellow"! Coriolan had always maintained that instead of composing sonatas or trios, I should have been writing books . . . Dear old Coriolan! Not only was that "instead of" totally unjustified, in fact the whole statement was no more than the expression of blind or deluded friendship. Perhaps I should have married some sweet, charming, dumb blonde who was easy to live with, even if she was penniless. I tried to picture myself languishing in a two-room flat together with screaming kids and a wife with faded looks: was that a preferable fate? Would that be any sweeter than the life of this still youthful, well-dressed young man, his face unmarked by worry or tiredness, bound hand and foot to a lovely apartment merely by the snares of an hysterical and silly woman? Would I be any more manly if I were killing myself working in some factory? Would I be any more proud of myself? Would my vanity be satisfied if – at best – I were giving piano lessons to snotty-nosed children in faceless apartment blocks, while an exhausted wife waited for me "at home", albeit a home I could call my own? I was not so sure. My pride did not lie there – nor did I associate it with that: not with virtue or effort. My pride lay in being happy, it was as simple as that! Quickly said, but it took a long time to admit: I was pleased with myself only when happy.

And now, being sad, I therefore felt humiliated and hurt.

Like all those who shy away from any knocks, like all emotional deserters, I had only to suffer the slightest wound and it became infected. Whatever I might decide, whatever I might succeed in doing with my life, I had first, and with the utmost urgency, to cleanse this wound, whether with lies, baseness or magnanimity. I had to reject all of that past and of the immediate present in order to rediscover if not happiness then at least the memory of happiness, the taste of it, and the desire for it. If not, I would no longer – not for a very long time – be able to think of that happiness, my happiness, without immediately adding the qualification "shameful".

I had entered the apartment without even slowing my pace as I passed the sitting-room, and I had gone straight to my studio via the servants' corridor, which I had never used so much as during these last few days. Before, my route had always automatically taken me past Laurence's sitting-room, her dressing-room, her bedroom, the nerve centre and emotional focus of the house. I had never previously thought of using this narrow cupboard-lined passageway that ran past a closed linen room, then a deserted kitchen, before reaching the little hallway dubbed "Odile's office"; and opening on to her office was my studio, once an old lumber room. An old lumber room – I realized with pointless regret, since my state of imprisonment had been a matter of time and not place – that must have had a service staircase, now blocked up, leading from it. In fact, it was not the constraints of a husband trying to escape his wife – hence tiresome, emotional constraints – that I should have had to put up with (had I really had to put up with any unpleasantness in my life, something I persistently doubted), but those of a young man giving his mother the slip. My mother had been very kind-hearted, perhaps a bit distant, but I much preferred her to a mother like Laurence: assuming that she would have loved me, I would have turned out sadistic and, or, impotent, had I been brought up by her.

And while on the subject of impotence, I asked myself a few questions: Laurence was not the kind of woman to dispense with my conjugal respects for very long. Did she think me capable of presenting them to her, as though performing some gymnastic exercise? Or – a more likely possibility – did she imagine, yet again and ever more erroneously, that our quarrel would arouse my desire? That anger would give an additional ardour to my embraces? Did she really believe that a man just robbed of his money is left titillated? Probably so, after all; it could not be her reasoning or her sporadic sentimentality but rather her bad faith that allowed her to envisage these optimistic outcomes. I could even count myself lucky that she had not said: "What are you talking about? Money? Bah! Pooh! No vulgarity, please!" I would have been left speechless, perhaps, and even impressed. Laurence, thank God, was so far from being aloof with regard to money that such an impudent remark would never have occurred to her. An absence of thought, or a happy oversight, but natural enough, after all . . . If one's own arguments spontaneously sprang to the minds of one's adversaries, there would be no further conflict. "And conflict would cease for want of combatants," declared the Monsieur Jourdain who had recently taken up residence in my mind, whilst the permanent occupant, myself, remained despondently silent.

The empty and silent house was dismal after the cheerful chaos at the races. Strange, at six o'clock. Unless the women, Laurence and Odile, afraid of my righteous anger, were cowering under the dining-table. Exhausted by Longchamp, I closed my eyes and almost fell asleep. It was quite by chance that I noticed an envelope on the ground that I must have sent flying with the bedcover; it was addressed to "Vincent". I immediately recognized Laurence's beautifully regular and legible handwriting, and I hesitated before opening it. What if she asked me in the letter to pack my bags, to disappear? For a moment I panicked: I should be lost, and she knew it . . . So I just stood there, looking at it, and all of a sudden the grotesqueness of my circumstances, the awfulness of my natural cowardice, and of the cowardice Laurence had developed in me, put me in a rage. I tore her envelope apart, rather than opened it. What I read in it was not my dismissal but an invitation, an order: "Vincent," she wrote, "don't forget we're dining at the Valances this evening. Your dinner-jacket is hanging up in the bathroom. Please wake me at seven. Until then, I simply *must* rest."

I was very irritated by it. First of all, because she had underlined "must", as though I were in the habit of disturbing her sleep; secondly, because dinner at the Valances, with her poshest friends, was an ordeal, especially after Longchamp. Irritated, yes, I was irritated by that letter, but extremely relieved to be no more than irritated; after all, I could very well not have been mistaken about its contents.

Chapter Eight

It was perhaps because he described himself as being born of an old Protestant family, and because the newspapers generally referred to him as a veteran of the Paris Bar that Maître Paul Valance seemed, at the age of seventy-two, so well preserved. As in fact did his wife, Mannie, fifteen years his junior, with whom he claimed to have been living for some thirty years now – which was true, although each of them invariably looked astounded by the accounts given by the other of their joint existence.

"Last week, in London, we met two Englishmen charged with duelling," Valance would say, for instance. And everyone would cry – but long after Mannie, the most astonished of all – "No! That can't be true!" Or Mannie would announce: "I saw that poor Jacqueline X get bitten by a puppy at the Plaza." And while everyone exclaimed, her husband's loud voice would rise above the babble: "What? Bitten? Jacqueline? But who bit her?" This of course held out the promise for their old age of more unpredictable and more amusing conversations than most, but also left one imagining Mannie, at some future date, hearing someone say in the course of a dinner: "That poor fellow Valance! I'd seen him only the day before! How sad!" And she crying out: "Pardon? My husband, dead? But what did he die of?"

The Valances had just the one son, Philibert, a retarded child, whom they had kept completely hidden away for twenty-five years, after which they had brought him out again and virtually readopted him: "Philibert said this, Philibert did that . . ." Since their rediscovery of him, they spoke of him with an emotionalism and enthusiasm that others with whom they came into contact found appalling or comic, depending on their character. Laurence, of course, believed them to be conscience-stricken and considered them disgraceful, as parents, but I, for my part, found them easier to explain. Childhood is a delightful, blessed state, but one that becomes all the more grotesque, in fact ghastly, when unduly prolonged. On the other hand, if this favoured condition returns a little too soon, it seems like a special privilege, something rather amusing. It is retardedness that humiliates parents, not precocity. The Valances had surely been despairing witnesses to their son's lack of development; from the age of ten until he reached adulthood, and even later, he would have "not yet matured". But having practically forgotten him after twenty-five years, they had been quite equal to rediscovering him, at thirty-five years of age, "already in his second childhood". His pathological infantilism had become psychological. And no doubt, for Philibert too, after twenty-five years of cruelty, sadness and loneliness, this triumphal return was a delight. He would come bounding up to me like a puppy, with shining eyes, as soon as I arrived, for I was the only person who spoke to him in his parents' absence. Showing even more friendliness than usual, Mannie came up to take my hands, and shook them.

"Ah, Vincent!" she said. "Did you know that Layton wants to photograph your wife, our lovely Laurence? He assured me she had an Etruscan profile! Can you imagine? Bill Layton doing a portrait of somebody at last!"

"He must be mad! How very kind!" exclaimed Laurence, who had blushed with happiness.

"Aren't you surprised, my dear Vincent?" Mannie had finally let go of my hands. "Aren't you surprised to have a wife with an Etruscan profile?"

Since I made no response, she went on:

"No, it doesn't amaze him. Nothing amazes him any more! Nothing surprises him any more!" she said, addressing the company at large, and for some incomprehensible reason everyone burst out laughing.

I bowed.

"Laurence will never cease to amaze me, my dear Mannie," I retorted, and I shot a glance at Laurence, who immediately averted her gaze.

I could see her in profile, tense and rigid with fear. It was curious to think that this woman who, only that afternoon, would have been able to take any disparaging remark of mine should, only two hours later, so dread the least hint of irony from me in public. It was true that the Valances' house was one of the few places were she could "breathe at my own rhythm", as she put it, and as I for a long time had put up with hearing her say, taking it as an expression of childish enthusiasm and not, as I now took it to be, the most snobbish kind of nonsense.

One way or another, our little – or huge – marital cloud did not prevent that evening at the Valances from being utterly delightful. The friendliness of the guests, the interest and curiosity they showed in one another, and particularly in me, were sufficiently rare to seem to me refreshing and even enjoyable. The Valances liked to prove their originality by the eclecticism of their guest list, ranging from a couple of actors who headed a charity organization to a dozy Academician, and including clients and industrialists with an interest in Fine Arts; not to mention several pretty young women, *a posteriori* evidence of the barrister's amorous energy.

So, Philibert, all scrubbed and neatly dressed, ageless but enduring, came in search of me, dragged me away from the sitting-room and led me into the smoking-room. With a wave of his hand, which had something of his father's grace about it, he invited me to sit in an armchair.

"Sit down!" he said in that hoarse voice of his.

Taller than me, he had dull eyes and hair of some indeterminate, yellowish, nut colour. I could very well imagine him bothering a woman on a street corner, and even raping her.

"Tell me," he said, "tell me . . ." And he began heaving with laughter . . . "Now . . . your money? Is it true? Have you got money?"

"How do you know? You want some money too, now, do you?"

"I know about it from my parents. Everyone says you've got money now."

Really! Even this innocent was interested in my fortune! I was less surprised that his parents should have welcomed me so warmly; and still less by the extraordinary kindness, the extraordinary heartiness of everyone I had spoken to since arriving. I was no longer Laurence's absent-minded husband, I was the rich composer of "Showers", I was a personality. And the money vultures here this evening were going to be rapidly eclipsed by the eagles or butterflies of success. I had until now been regarded as Laurence's vassal, her husband and parasite. Today, I could see all too clearly, I was enthroned suzerain lord, consort, a person of responsibility! They were unaware that I was already nothing more than some vague supernumerary, about to be shown the door . . . These respectful looks and glances I was receiving, new to me as they were, were no longer valid.

"Do you want to see your painting?" asked Philibert.

For the Valances had a marvellous collection of Impressionists that the husband's flair for such things had enabled him to buy for a song, so he said (but, given the period, I feared they must have cost him many more songs than flair). There were two Manets, a Renoir, a Vuillard, and there in a corner my favourite: a Pissarro that showed a village in the foreground, with rounded hills behind, in that apple-green of children's drawings, with a soft, clear light reigning over them, the triumphant light of high summer. A light that in this picture caught the ears of corn like a shock of hair, tossed them back and stroked them, all in one direction. As it had crimped the treetops, now standing to attention beneath their lacquered manes; as it had checked and suborned with flashes of brilliance and silver a river yet impatient for the sea. One had the impression that it was the light that had sketched out this innocent, rudimentary landscape just before Pissarro arrived and recreated it as it was: perfectly still. Its stillness as spurious and alluring as that eternity it seemed at once to represent and to promise ... I had adored many paintings in my life, often more subtle, more complicated or crazier than this, but what I liked about it was that it gave me an image of happiness, and most of all, a happiness that was accessible.

"Have you come to see your Pissarro?"

I turned round. The veteran of the Paris Bar had just come into the smoking-room and was both offering me a glass and inviting me to take a seat, he too with a gracious gesture. I sat down gingerly: I was beginning to be wary of smoking-rooms and of those who frequented them ...

"Well, my dear Vincent?" said Valance with a big smile. And I was horrified to realize that I had not seen him and his wife since my "hit" and that I was bound to be treated to congratulations on it during dinner. I raised my hand.

"We'll talk about it later, Paul, if you don't mind."

"As you wish! As you wish! But meanwhile, if you still like it as much as before, I would be delighted to sell you this little Pissarro, for it is a 'little' one, you know! I bought it in a sale at Sotheby's; it wasn't very much. As you also know, I wouldn't try to make a profit at your expense ..."

I returned his smile, but I was secretly sorry that it was not one of the many paintings he had bought for a song. It was just my luck it had to come from Sotheby's! Ah, well! Valance had rested his hand on my shoulder as he paced the room.

"No, I wouldn't want to take any of that lovely new money of yours, my dear old friend!" (He smiled.) "I look upon you a little as my son, you know."

But at that moment his gaze fell on Philibert, who was walking in front of us, lopsidedly, and Valance added very quickly:

"Well ... I look upon you as *a* son ..."

Which was very adroit from a social point of view, but from the paternal point of view, appalling. As a matter of fact, he blushed, glanced round anxiously, as though he might have been overheard, then, reassured, he led me to the door.

"Come," he said, "we must sit down to eat. Our last guest has arrived. Do you know her? Viviane Bellacour. A charming widow!" he added, squeezing my arm lightly and giving me a roguish look.

It was the first time since I had known him that Valance had made a saucy allusion, and I realized that, in these circles, my financial success had conferred on me, as well as respectability and interest, a newfound virility. Not that secret and necessitous – almost domestic – virility required of me, vis-à-vis Laurence, by the conditions of our marriage; but an acquired masculinity that gave me the right, indeed the duty, to look around me, and upon their own women, with lustful gaze. A gaze that would have been forbidden to me before, because I was poor; a gaze that, without my realizing it, would have made me then, throughout those seven years, the wicked black man for these whites. Then, I might have been practically lynched, and I congratulated myself in retrospect on having nonetheless shared with them their lovely white women before being granted – along with the acknowledgement of my wealth – the right to do so. This would provide me with a few consolatory memories at some later date, once my ruination had come to light. For I had a fairly strong suspicion that, as far as these men were concerned, my wealth had been too short-lived to command any lasting respect from them. It was not enough to be grasping, you also had to be tight-fisted; or, to put it another way, it was not enough to be smart, you also had to be shrewd. In short, it was not enough to be rich, you had to stay rich!

The sitting-room had filled with guests in our absence. First, I saw two friends of Laurence, with whom I'd had a brief but close acquaintance (if one may thus describe a little writhing in the dark with a woman who wants obscurity, anonymity, secrecy and at the same time passionate declarations of love). Each of them had a man at her side whom I at once recognized as their husbands, before they were even introduced to me. They complained of the time difference between Paris and New York, and confided to me: "We do a lot of travelling!" – while I nodded and muttered under my breath, "I know, I know! Why don't you carry on, then!" As for their wives, they had that funny look women have in such circumstances: a worried look, their lover's opinion of their husband being of greater concern to them than the reverse . . . which, generally speaking, is unlikely to be available. Having recently found common cause with husbands, I made a pretence of being extremely impressed by these two.

Laurence was deep in conversation with the Academician, who had grown weary of everything, apparently, except good food, for he kept darting anxious glances at the door to the dining-room. The young widow was too blonde, too suntanned, but very beautiful, with that misty, rather drunken look in her eye typical of women deprived of men for too long. She cast worried glances now at Valance, now at his son, obviously saying to herself, not without some sadness: "Two late for him now! And too soon, as it always will be, for the other!" It was no doubt for this reason that she gave me a sexy wink, whilst my two former mistresses of brief duration, inflamed by our shared memories, were also making eyes at me that same evening. I went from being cast as a gigolo to playing Prince Charming, a Prince Charming honour-bound to spread himself thin, if he was to appear polite.

At the table, I found myself seated on Mannie's left, the place on her right being reserved, all the same, for the French Academy.

"I had to put Waldo on my right," Mannie said to me, greatly embarrassed, as though I had not, at her dinners to date, invariably been seated at the end of the table, or next to Philibert if they were a woman short.

"It's the price of being young," she went on, "but believe me, it's a small price to pay, and, your dear old Mannie aside, you aren't so badly placed."

True enough, on my left, the young widow was unfolding her napkin with long, carnivorous fingernails, and a little further down the table, on the same side as I was seated, and therefore unable to keep her eye on me, I saw Laurence ensconced between Valance and one of the industrialist husbands. I slipped my legs under the long tablecloth, trailing down to the ground as usual, and I sighed in anticipation. Meals at the Valances never ran to fewer than five courses.

"You know, you're better in the flesh!" said the widow next to me without any preamble, and for a moment I was at a loss for words.

"Better in the flesh?"

"Yes, better than in the photographs."

"What photographs?"

Viviane looked embarrassed. (The poor woman's name was Viviane.)

"I haven't read the other papers," she apologized, "I'm only referring to today's."

And since I still looked surprised, she gave me a wary look and said irritably:

"You have read today's *Le Soir*, haven't you?"

"No, why?"

Stretching across my plate, she leant over to Mannie:

"Mannie, this gentleman, the one sitting next to me, claims not to have seen this evening's paper!"

"It's quite possible," said Mannie indulgently with a smile, "he's so absent-minded! You haven't shown it to him, Laurence?"

There was a note of reproach in her voice (as though she and her husband always told each other everything!). Laurence leant across the table and gave me a lack-lustre, sidelong glance.

"I didn't have time," she said. "He was still asleep at eight . . ."

"But I have it, I've kept it," Valance chanted, jokingly and ironically playing the fan, at least to the extent of getting up and going to fetch the newspaper in question himself. He came back brandishing it, and handed it to me, open at the relevant page. I had the surprise of seeing myself spread across three columns, sitting alone on a café terrace, which it took me a good ten seconds to recognize as Le Fouquet's. The article was headlined: "The new Midas of music finds his inspiration on café terraces."

"Midas! Midas!" He certainly had a way with words, this reporter, he was truly inspired! Midas or Job, I just could not bring myself to admit that this blurred individual with a stupid, slightly befuddled expression was me. Once I had been convinced of this, I immediately, instinctively, searched for the figure of Jeannine, to the right of me in the photograph, slightly further along the pavement, where I had seen her and accosted her . . . but she wasn't there. Well, she had not yet arrived, and in my agitation I almost turned to the next page.

"Are you admiring yourself? You really hadn't seen yourself, Vincent?" said Mannie's voice, and I looked up.

She was smiling at me, meltingly, and I understood the second motive for that welcome, for Valance's interest in me, the offer of the Pissarro, the remembrance of the women, and the conspiratorial looks of those around me: I had acquired not only riches, which was not so very difficult, but, of much more importance, fame. What am I saying? Stardom!

"No, I hadn't seen it. I really didn't know about it."

I sought Laurence's gaze, but in vain. There were five people between us.

"In any case, Laurence had read it!" Mannie informed me, in a more perfidious manner than usual. "Go on, read what she said! It's delicious . . . delicious . . ."

I leant forward and saw that the inset in the middle of the page was not the photo of some journalist but of Laurence herself. It was a very good photograph in fact, which she must have given to the journalist at the same time as this invaluable information: " 'It's on café terraces that my husband usually finds his musical inspiration,' we were told by the charming Laurence, wife of the musician who so rapidly found fame with 'Showers', the song that has brought him a veritable deluge of dollars ..." etc. etc.

I hurriedly folded up the newspaper. I had half-expected the journalist to add: "It's also on café terraces, and in the arms of prostitutes, that the musician spends his afternoons." But no, this reporter was a decent sort – discreet or, if not, constrained to be.

"Laurence!" cried Mannie. "Your Vincent is playing it cool: he hasn't even read his article to the end!"

"My article!" It was "my article" now! I had composed a little jingle that was probably already getting on their nerves and which, according to Xavier Bonnat, was not even mine. I was a gigolo, perhaps a plagiarist, but no matter: I had acquired a lot of money and I had "my" photograph in "the" newspaper. The crowd could not but defer to me.

The rest of the article was worthy of the beginning: "Strolling through Paris ... brooding walks ... his loving wife ... the beautiful Laurence ... for ten years ... married ... twenty-two ... a life devoted to work and privacy ... his Steinway ..." It was dreadful.

"It's dreadful," I said under my breath, and I let the newspaper fall to the ground without another word.

"You should be rather pleased, shouldn't you?" the widow next to me whispered in a low, reproving voice.

Like everyone present, she was vaguely shocked by my ingratitude towards the press. To complain about being famous was certainly considered good form, but to do so one needed a little more than a single article to one's credit, albeit three columns. One needed to have held pride of place in numerous newspapers and journals to be entitled to clamour fretfully for a private life and a little decorum on the part of the public.

"I'm very pleased to be sitting next to you, and that's that," I said firmly.

Startled, she drew back from the table, and I suddenly felt enormous desire for her. Viviane was pretty, or almost pretty: there was nothing natural about her – her hair, her gestures, her complexion, her body, the pitch of her voice – but I desired her, just like that, to be revenged. Except that, completely illogically, I did not want Laurence to come upon us. I simply had to have this woman before the evening was over; to reassure myself, to reassure the oafish, primitive man that I was, lacking in all subtlety, and suddenly a little too disgusted by everything, and above all by his own fame.

"You know, you ought to sing, Viviane!" I said, full of fervour and conviction. "With your voice, what a waste!"

And I pressed my knee against hers without the slightest ambiguity, at the same time gazing at her intently. She coughed, covered her face with her napkin and emerged from behind it looking pink beneath her fake tan (she had not moved her leg).

"You think so?" she exclaimed in a shrill voice. "I've been told that before. But coming from you . . . I have to admit . . ."

I smiled at her and behaved grossly for the rest of the meal. I used my left hand to cut my meat, drink my wine and to lay stress on the few words I spoke; the other hand, under Viviane's dress, seduced her modesty and played havoc with her senses. At one point, seated on the edge of her chair, she stopped dead in midsentence, and blenched, leant over the table and rested the entire top part of her body against it, her head bent forward, her eyes half-closed, chewing her lower lip with a kind of inaudible yelping. I remained quite still; like the others sitting near her, I gave her a polite look of surprise. She recovered herself after a few seconds and I marvelled at the capacity of women to seize in passing the crudest pleasure, to make an exhibition of it almost, and all with such naturalness. I returned my hand to the table, she straightened up again, opened her eyes and settled back into her chair, her gaze scarcely more flustered than her voice.

"Forgive me," she said to the humanitarian actor who was leaning towards her and thinking perhaps of giving her the benefit of his medical experience. "Forgive me! I have the most awful pain in my liver every now and again. Right there!" she added, pointing to her waist with her beringed hand.

"There? That's the pancreas!" he stated emphatically.

For although he raised funds mostly for cancer, his compassion had little by little devolved and there was now nothing in the human body that escaped his diagnosis or his charitable zest.

"Do you already have plans for your little fortune, my dear Vincent?" Valance asked me from afar with a kindly smile.

I caught a glimpse of the gratified amusement on Laurence's face, and promptly wished that she had been under the table for a moment, five minutes ago ... But Viviane's pleasure had been relaxing for me too, and I now felt only the faintest desire to revenge myself, a desire faint enough to let me venture to do so calmly.

"Oh, so Laurence hasn't said anything to you?"

Valance assumed a look of surprise, his guests too.

"No? Well now, what a secretive person she is! My royalties are going straight into the bank, in Laurence's name – the money that has already come in, and the money to come. We decided that by mutual consent."

"You mean, we've opened a joint account," Laurence corrected me in a cold voice, but I cut in:

"Yes, well, all the cheques have my signature on them already, as you can imagine, and are in her bag. By what right would I keep a centime for myself after all this time? You're well placed to know how much I owe my wife," I said with a flourish. And seizing Mannie's hand, a hand as inert as she, I kissed it piously.

But her fingers remained still and frozen beneath my lips. There was a moment's astonishment, then pity: there was no doubt about it, unknown or famous, either way the boy was a fool.

"I know, I know, it seems a bit excessive," I went on, good-humouredly. "After all, a million dollars ... Even if Laurence spoiled me dreadfully for seven years, I still didn't cost her seven million old francs a month. Far from it! Let's not exaggerate. Is that not true, my darling?"

And I gave an affectionate laugh. The silence of the guests had become total and more than heavy. Although they all worked it out in their heads, my calculation struck them as being in the worst possible taste, and thoroughly outlandish. Since when did a gigolo refund his mistress (or his wife)? And since when did he bother about the difference between his debts and how much of them he repaid? No one could really make any sense of it.

"No, no, no, never that much, I swear it," I said confidently, and I directed a look laden with virtuousness and pride at Laurence, who sat there stoically with a strained smile on her lips.

"No, of course not," she agreed in a low voice, but without looking at me.

Had it even occurred to her? Or was Odile the only one with the slightest head for figures in our cosy nest on boulevard Raspail?

"And another thing: 'Showers' – you know, that tune from the film *Showers* . . . I hope you know it?"

"Certainly, yes, yes! Certainly!" said the Academician, suddenly awake, who stared at me from behind his glasses with fascinated eyes.

"Well, I can tell you that Laurence wrote half of 'Showers' . . ."

Another silence. Laurence raised her hand.

"No," she whispered, "no!"

But I raised my voice.

"Yes, yes! I was strumming on the piano, trying to work out a tune. I had just the first two notes, the chord, if you like, yes: doh-ray . . . And then who should come along and sing all the rest in one great burst: fah, me, lah, soh, lah, doh, ray – no, that's wrong, lah, doh, fah, ray? [I'm not very good at musical notation, no matter what Laurence may say . . .] No, without her, there would be no 'Showers', no film music, no dollars!"

And since Valance was staring at me incredulously, I concluded:

"Guess what the first present was that Laurence bought me with our money (actually, her money, now)? A Steinway piano, a huge thing! What I've always dreamed of!"

And pausing there, I gazed round at all the guests with a look of triumph that Philibert was alone in returning. With a sigh I turned my attention to my vanilla custard. I had always adored vanilla custard and I was pleased that Mannie had remembered. I told her so. She nodded slowly, looking more irritated than pleased by my compliments, and very quickly rose from the table, thereby giving the signal, after all that silence, for a joyful hubbub. I hardly had time to finish my dessert, still less to savour it.

Chapter Nine

Without thinking, I turned on the radio in the car on the way home, to break the silence. I had ended up drinking numerous brandies with the husband of one of my temporary mistresses, a good-looking fellow who had turned out to be very congenial, for a businessman. So much so, it was a wonder that his wife had cheated on him with me . . . Anyhow, we had decided to see each other again, and after some pious and woolly talk about meeting to do something athletic, we had agreed on a game of dice at a bar near the Madeleine. I certainly had experienced the most disparate emotions that evening: having felt those associated with aesthetics and stardom, eroticism and comedy, I had also tasted the pleasures of ridicule, of feeling ridiculous and making a fool of oneself, and I have to say, these were not the least of pleasures. Furthermore, I was now familiar with the agreeableness of male esteem.

It was obvious, looking at Laurence's profile, that her evening had not been as rich an experience as mine. So I had turned on the radio, but – after some good jazz – only to light upon the beginning of "Showers", played by a saxophonist who introduced some superb variations into it. Suddenly I felt proud of myself: my music was inventive, fluent, pure. It was self-evident but without being in the least bit facile, and I was surprised, a little late in the day, that I had let someone else take the credit for it. Even if the fruits of it went elsewhere, it belonged to me, it was the only thing that truly belonged to me and to no one else but me, since it had come out of my head, my musings, my memory and my musical imagination. There was nothing anyone could do to alter that. Only, its arrival on the airwaves that evening was badly timed – as though I was being deliberately provocative (and as though I were in charge of programming on Radio-Musique). What with Laurence and Coriolan, who must curse my foolishness every time "Showers" happened to come on the air between the results of the first and second race, I was not exactly surrounded by an enthusiastic claque.

I was worried about Coriolan. How was I to help him survive now or later, once our seventy thousand francs had been frittered away at Longchamp or elsewhere? Yet race courses were among the only places where one could run through money in the most agreeable way, or even make it yield a profit, as I had proved that afternoon. Unfortunately, as sure as I had been of winning when I arrived there today, I was equally sure of eventually losing it all, somewhere or other, sooner or later. I was, like many people, a sensible gambler, contrary to the opinion of those peculiar tribes that do not gamble, and who in their conformism invariably imagine the gambler before a race course or the green baize as someone wilfully shipwrecked, thousands of leagues from dry land. In this, these defective sages are mistaken, for no one is as hard on himself and as apprehensive at the outset as a real gambler, so much in danger does he feel. Only at the outset, for dry land appears to him increasingly detached from any real continent, and daily life from any sweetness. Until the day when, through an incomprehensible reversal, the only dry land to be trusted, being the only uncertain ground, lies beneath a horse's hoofs, and real life beneath the gambling-chips of a casino, nothing in the end having proved more arduous and more cruel than daily life. Finally, to conclude the celebration of this vice, there is nothing brighter and cleaner than the colours of jockeys' caps or those of gambling-chips; there is nothing more varied than a race course in the open air, or the smoke-filled room of a gambling-den; there is nothing lighter than the tread of a thoroughbred or the weight of a million-franc chip. Similarly, there is no more decent way to signal your triumph or ruin than by turning over two cards. I had a sudden desire to gamble, just as I had felt a sudden desire for Viviane a little while ago: it was irresistible. I felt my heartbeat slowed with the flux of sluggish but hectic blood, despotic blood that I no longer recognized as mine, perhaps through having diluted it so much with boredom.

"Stop right here, please," I said.

Laurence braked so suddenly that I banged my forehead on the windscreen.

"I feel like gambling," I added. "You see? Up there. Just up there."

And I pointed with my chin to the upstairs floor, where, I knew, tables and cards awaited me. But seeing her tense face, I felt sorry for her and said:

"Come. Come if you like. Come, it's fun."

She did not answer, she did not stir, as though petrified by my eagerness. I got out, slammed the door and walked round the car. The pavement swayed beneath my feet. I leant in at the window.

"Drive carefully! I'll be home soon."

From the side of the road I watched her, ever cautious, test the headlights, the side-lights, switching them on and off once or twice, then she drove away without a word, without a glance. Before she had disappeared from view, I had done an about-turn and bounded off to the club.

I shall not recount in detail my vicissitudes that night: suffice to say, they were spectacular. I was lent as much as I wanted against the club's bank-cheque, and, I imagine, thanks to that famous article. For five hours I lost frightening sums of money, which I virtually won back at dawn. So I walked away at daybreak, without a sou, but brimming with pride and happiness. I had very nearly lost a fortune, but I had not given way to pessimism, I had fought back, and I had acquitted myself handsomely. I was proud of myself, possessed with an exultation that no one but a gambler would have been able to understand. To do so required the knowledge that a gambler's reckoning is never expressed in the present indicative but in the past conditional, and that it was not "I lost this much . . ." that came into my mind but "I could have lost that much . . .", the optimistic conjugations of gambling being not the least of its charms.

So I walked back from the Opéra to the Lion de Belfort. In that tardy dawn, banks of mist were still stealing under the bridges, silently, like thieves. And Paris resembled a sleeping woman, unwary and beautiful. And there was no city in the world more beautiful, and not a happier man than me.

It was seven, or just about, when I got to the top of boulevard Raspail, home – what I tried to call home even though there was already a bedroom inside that was no longer mine. Yet maybe it would strike me, even so, as an unwarranted intrusion if Laurence interfered with my old studio. As was the case whenever I left a house, it would not be the private rooms I regretted most. For a start, the sense of being in my own home was something I had felt only in my parents' house, the house where I had spent eighteen years: at home – that's to say, theirs and at the same time mine. At my father's funeral – he died after my mother – I had mourned twice over, both for him and for our house in rue Doublet, which was going to belong to others. But this sense that I was only passing through was one I had experienced everywhere, except in a hotel room where I had lived for six years, a room that I was amazed and horrified to see occupied by someone other than me when I returned there. Today, I wondered about this apartment where, if I had not felt at home, at least I had felt myself to be a life tenant. If things turned out badly, I already knew that I would never again be able to go past boulevard Raspail without a sense of exile or feeling there was some mistake. That said, it was my own fault, I had only myself to blame. I should never have forgotten that a person is never at home anywhere. And that between a freestone apartment block and one of these mortal creatures that we are, the relationship can never be anything but one of power, and of unequal power. The brutality of money is more categorical with regard to property than anything else: either you own it or you have to be ready to leave.

I had breakfast at the Lion de Belfort, which had scarcely opened. And I watched with awe those men standing at the bar, still half-asleep and in a hurry, who were off to work for the day, those men, in fact, who led a normal life. My spirits sank: in six months I had written one chartbuster, earned then lost a fortune, and I was on the verge of being thrown out by my wife. What was to become of me? This question, having been buried in oblivion for seven years, now confronted me far more starkly than it had then. It was no use my casually dismissing it at every hour of the day, I could not prevent my reason from occasionally shouting in my ears: "What's going to happen to you? How will you live? Where? What will you do? What can you do? How will you cope with work and a hard life?" So it was with some anxiety that I returned to the flat. I went past Laurence's bedroom, my frame of mind that of a penniless tenant. I walked on tiptoe, breathing quietly, as when I had owed a few weeks' rent to the owner of my hotel in the Latin Quarter.

Once in bed, I was reluctant to take stock of the situation. Apart from the fact that it was something that did not agree with me, I could already guess the outcome: if I thought long and hard, if I drew up a list of my faults and grievances, and those of Laurence, a logical assessment of our acts, I was bound to come off best. But if it was a question of sentiment, my victory, I knew, would be but cold comfort.

It was pointless and futile to sum up or write down what had happened, and to draw conclusions: except that I did not feel guilty, I had never felt guilty, since the outbreak of hostilities, of anything but frivolousness. The list of charges against Laurence was more substantial, revealing at least an element of premeditation, which was not in my file.

In my narrow bed in the dark, unable to sleep, I switched on the radio. I happened to tune in to Beethoven's septet, which cleansed my mind of everything, and by the end left me feeling vulnerable, adolescent, on the verge of tears. It was a mistake to listen to this music; it contained all that anyone would want to know about love: attentive gentleness, passionate gaiety, and especially tenderness, and that unwavering trust. All that we had never known, and of which we would only ever possess the illusion, the semblance – more often than not of our own laborious making; more often than not, too, at the wrong time. That love of which we could claim no great experience except insofar as one of us had believed in it longer, been more hurt by it, or brought to it more trust and vulnerability than the other. That love, in short, which it was so shameful not to have felt and so heart-breaking not to have inspired. In a word, love . . . which had nothing to do with the pantomime staged by Laurence, and so painful to me. It was that love, retold in the night by a bassoon, a clarinet and a cello, amongst others, that made me sentimental and weak and sad.

The day was dawning, it was light, and I was still awake. Without flamboyance, impudence and frivolity, I came face to face with myself, a poor fool who had thought to escape society and whom in the end society despised, just as his own wife did, a poor fool who was going to wind up in the gutter, reduced to a single friend – an alcoholic, at that; a poor fool who'd had two lucky breaks, not made the most of them, and was now destined for the worst, as far as he was concerned: in other words, poverty and humiliation. I lay on my bed, exhausted, defenceless, and, I thought, lucid. As ever, like everyone else, I felt as lucid in my pessimism as I mistrusted myself when happy. Yet I knew perfectly well that the worst was not inevitable, it just seemed inevitable. But that night I did not remember any of those wise sayings. I lapsed easily into despair and the anguish of a guilty conscience – especially as these crises were, with me, so infrequent that their very rarity gave them an aura of truthfulness.

Yet – and I was well aware of this – at the root of my despair there was, in the first place, myself; a self lacking in strength, trust, levity; an infantile self, pusillanimous and mediocre, with whom I was much more angry than with the fact of actually being alive, since there was another self within me who usually made my life so delightful.

I fell asleep only with the first rays of sunshine.

I woke up with a monumental hangover, which at once reminded me of the cognacs the night before and left me feeling vaguely guilty. Vaguely anxious too, as though Laurence still had the right to punish me. Oddly, I could not imagine my life without penalties imposed by her. Worse, I felt a kind of nostalgia for them. Maybe my equilibrium lay in the disequilibrium between the violence of her feelings and the nebulousness of mine. And maybe I blamed her less for becoming extreme and dangerous than for not being a counterbalance to me any more, a guarantee of my security. To put it more simply, I could not believe that she could desire my presence as much as all that, a presence without any sense of attachment on my part. Be that as it may, I felt sorry for myself that morning and dreamed of an entente cordiale. I would not be able to endure for much longer these sarcastic remarks, these gibes and this bitterness, I would not be able to tolerate this atmosphere. I got up, dressed quickly, played a few notes on the piano, struck and held two or three chords a few times to relax myself, and finally telephoned Coriolan at the café. He was there; probably recounting our day at the races, for I could hear the heroic ring in his voice on the phone.

"I'm running late."

He laughed and I realized he was drunk.

"Come over here!" I said abruptly. "Come on over! I want to talk to you about the Steinway, and I haven't even got you to listen to it yet. Besides, I've lots of things to tell you."

There was silence.

"But . . . what about Laurence?"

"What difference can that make? I'm already in such a pretty pass! And anyway, she's out," I added valiantly. And I could hear from his breathing that this allayed his reservations, too.

Five minutes later, we were in my studio, and Odile, the

poor innocent, delighted by this unexpected development, made us coffee while the Steinway reverberated with our chords.

"What a tone!" Coriolan was overcome with admiration. "Everything sounds so marvellous on this piano. What's that you're playing now, for instance?"

"It's nothing," I said, "just two chords. It's the Steinway that makes them sound like a overture."

"Are you going to take it with you?"

"That depends on where we live. We won't be able to do any midnight flits with it."

Coriolan whinnied with glee at this idea, and Odile, who had until then been admiring his noble profile, was startled at the sight of those big teeth and that jovial face. She spilt some coffee on the floor, gave a shriek, and went off to fetch a floor-cloth from the kitchen.

"How many lashes of the whip do you get for something like that?" Coriolan enquired compassionately. "What are you doing down there, wiping the floor like a slave? A lovely creature like you, Odile, really! I imagine Her Royal Highness in any case is no easy taskmaster, and now with the favourite leaving it's going to be dreadful."

Odile nodded. She seemed as convinced as Coriolan of my imminent departure, and it scared me. They were rushing things!

"Not to worry, Odile, I have yet to deliver my last word on the matter!"

I had taken on a manly voice, but I saw them both lower their eyes and I was stung. I had to leave, they were surely right. At once. Besides, the question was not when to go, but where. And even then, it was not the lack of a destination that worried me, but the idea of packing my bags.

"And that last word will be quickly said!" I added firmly, as though to conclude the previous sentence. "Farewell! That won't take me long."

Their expressions of relief daunted me. What had I let myself in for? Of course, it was out of the question that I should forgive Laurence all the things she had done to me:

stolen my money, humiliated me, treated me like a servant, made a fool of me, and goodness knows what else ... Yet, like a sign of flagging pride, the indecisiveness of all my reactions bothered me. I realized full well I should not have been taking it all so calmly. Besides, I had shown my mettle only yesterday at the Valances. I had just to wait a while, and a rush of anger was bound to galvanize me, from one moment to the next. I tried to work myself up into a fury, but my hangover from the night before put up strong, stubborn resistance. I felt a surge of ill-temper towards Coriolan and Odile, and all their like. Why were they in such a hurry, so demanding? If I had listened to them, my behaviour would have always been, or should have been, exemplary, clear-cut, the kind of behaviour that poisons or blights your existence. Whatever happened, I refused to despise myself; I refused to join that dismal, ever-increasing, motley crowd of those who saw in me only a parasite or a cretin. If there was only one person left on this earth to appreciate me, I would be that person!

If Laurence's father was to be believed, even seven years ago I was not worthy of her. I knew at the time that a man did not automatically become worthy of a woman from the moment he made love to her adequately. But now I also knew that a woman who adequately supported a man did not automatically become worthy of him either. Only, Laurence was not aware of this axiom, or pretended not to be. Yet that was the problem, and it was the essential problem, every other a mere corollary: that I very nearly freed myself was one of these corollary problems; that she had prevented me, another; and that I ought to be taking it badly, a third.

Whatever the answers, I continued regularly to be seized with the conviction, even the positive certainty, that I had only to put Laurence across my knees and spank her bottom to set our marriage to rights again. Maybe this was not true. Maybe this hunch, too, was stupid and discreditable. What did I know about it? And what did I know of life? Nothing. Less and less. Nothing. Increasingly, nothing. The whole of life was uncertain, tiresome and ridiculous. Everything bored me. I had only one desire: to sleep, to take an aspirin and sleep . . . And I was expected to change my life – something of which, if the worst came to the worst, I was capable; but if that meant having to pack my bags, well, in that case . . . it was completely beyond me.

"Tell me," said Coriolan, "isn't there anything to drink in your Napoléon III drawing-room?"

Having dutifully sipped his coffee, he now felt legally authorized to continue his alcoholic odyssey.

"Why do you say that?" I asked.

"Because your furniture is Napoléon III, old man. Didn't you know? Really, you might have glanced at it, in seven years! It was of course your wife who took care of the drawing-room? The in-te-ri-or de-co-ra-tion!" he said, clearly enunciating each syllable.

While talking, we had come to the famous drawing-room, and I opened the drinks cabinet, took out a bottle and two glasses. Coriolan had sat down on the settee, making it creak, and was already smiling at the bottle. It was at that moment that we heard the doorbell ring and Odile's voice in the hall.

"Monsieur Chatel!" she said very loudly, to warn us. "Monsieur Chatel! What a pleasant surprise!"

This was all we needed – my father-in-law had arrived! I hastily handed my full glass to Coriolan and sat down opposite him, with my knees together like a schoolboy. A thieving schoolboy. Which was clear proof that I had never felt at home in this place, that I had never been my own master here.

"Is my daughter not in?" said the booming voice of that crook of a father-in-law.

I suddenly remembered he had stolen everything I possessed, and took some courage from this. But already he was entering the room like a raging bull, giving me a casual glance – which riled me – and staring at Coriolan, who had made himself comfortable.

"Monsieur . . .?"

"Señor!" said Coriolan, getting to his feet and simultaneously rising to his full height of 1.98 metres, dressed – only then did I notice – in an expensive mourning-suit. I had, in fact, given him a black suit for my wedding, which he had worn on only two other occasions: when his ironmonger died, and for some strange ceremony at the École des Beaux-Arts. I also noticed that he made an extremely good impression, as my father-in-law gave him a small, almost respectful, nod.

"Monsieur Chatel, Señor Latello!" I said, doubling the Ls and stressing the O – "of the Latelot family, who for generations have had a removal business in the 14th arrondissement. Monsieur Chatel is my wife's father," I said to Coriolan, "and Monsieur Latello is here on behalf of the Gramophono company, in Madrid, regarding my song rights."

"Monsieur!" said my father-in-law, with a gleam in his eye at the thought of an imminent deal.

"Señor!" said Coriolan, and he took a step forward, but my father-in-law did not retreat.

I admired the courage beneath his ruthlessness. I might have been afraid that he would recognize Coriolan as the deplorable drunk and skirt-chaser who had created a scandal at his daughter's wedding, but at the time he had only glimpsed in the semi-darkness the recumbent figure of a tipsy individual – dishevelled, rumpled and, what's more, full of mirth – a million miles from the Spanish gentleman seated on the settee in boulevard Raspail.

"El padre de la señora Laurens?"

Coriolan took my father-in-law's hand and held it in his own.

"Si," mumbled the poor man, *"Si! Yo soy* . . . uh . . . *je suis* . . . I am *el padre de* . . . my daughter! You know her?"

"Si, si, la conozco! Ah, bueno! Aquí es el padre y aquí es el marito! Bueno!" (Coriolan, the fool, had assumed a look of wonder as he seized the pair of us by the shoulder; both squeezed against his sides, we struggled desperately not to come face to face with each other across his chest.) *"Povres bougros!"* Coriolan continued to exclaim. *"Si, si, si!"* he went

on. "*La conozco! La conozco!*" And he freed us, not without giving each of us an exaggeratedly manly pat on the back that sent us both reeling.

"It's a great pity," said my father-in-law, a little shaken, and automatically dusting himself down, "it's a great pity that I don't speak Spanish! *No hablo!*"

And at the same time, just like a lot of ignoramuses, he gave Coriolan a smug, conspiratorial smile, as though his ignorance of the language spoken by the other were an innocent charm, irresistible to the latter.

"*No hablo,* but I have been twice" – "*Dos!*" [he said, waving two fingers in front of Coriolan] – "for reasons . . . well, never mind that! . . . and I know your famous toast: "*Amor, salud y pesetas, y tiempo para gustarlas!*" he said, humming and hawing.

(But when did he not hum and haw?)

"A toast? Bravo! Bravo! A toast!" cried Coriolan with delight. "A toast!"

And he picked up the bottle of whisky and immediately poured a large glass for my father-in-law and for me, not forgetting himself in the least.

"*Si, si!*" he said, brandishing his glass. "*Amor, salud y pesetas, y tiempo para gustarlas! Exactemente! Ecco!*"

"*Exactemente! Exactemente!*" said my father-in-law in tones of praise – whether intended for Coriolan for knowing his own language, or himself for having retained a few words of it, it was impossible to tell. "*Exactemente!*" he repeated, and not wanting to speak to me, he fell back on addressing his remarks to no one in particular.

"Ultimately, all languages are alike, everything comes from Latin, it's simple. It should not be forgotten that the whole of Europe spoke Latin, or Celtic. But sit down, Señor Latello, please!" And with an expansive gesture, as though master of the house, he invited him to take a seat on the wretched Napoléon III settee. "Are you here on business, Señor Latelio!" asked my father-in-law in a covetous voice.

"Late*ll*o, two Ls, Late*ll*o, *dos* L," said Coriolan. "Late*llio*!"

"Latelo! Latellio!" mumbled my father-in-law edgily.

"No, no! Late*ll*io! Late*ll*io! Lio, lio, lio!" Coriolan corrected him, adding three or four Ls, and I gave him a stern look.

It was time he stopped this doubling of consonants and that we brought to an end this farce that was already set to go wrong and, if Laurence arrived, was going to turn into a drama.

"Señor Latello," I said firmly, "*por el vuestro telefono, es aquí!*" And I drew him by the sleeve to the door.

My father-in-law automatically got to his feet, bowed, and impatiently – and, it already seemed to me, with dawning mistrust – watched us leave.

"*Yo ritorno! Yo ritorno!*" Coriolan called back to him from the door, but he was beginning to crack up, and he had hardly reached the staircase when he exploded.

He bellowed with laughter all the way down, pummelling me, like a schoolboy. We were just in time: from the lift going up as we were coming down, I caught the smell, as it passed us, of my wife's heavy perfume, a perfume too old for her, worn by whores and society women. The explanations upstairs, between father and daughter, following the sudden disappearance of a certain Spanish nobleman, Señor Latello, were not going to be devoid of interest. Unfortunately, we would not be there to enjoy them. I was still laughing at this prank of ours, but my return home would be less comic. And this thought must have been legible on my face because Coriolan scowled and, grabbing me by the shirt, he shook me.

"Let me remind you that she stole your money and made everyone take you for a nonentity. And whilst you may have made her father take me, your only friend, for a caballero, I swear to you, it's of no consequence! I swear to you, in the dirty tricks stakes you're way behind . . ."

He abruptly released me, and strode off towards the gateway. I stood there speechless for a moment. I understood what he was saying, of course, but how could I explain to him that if I was actually behind in the dirty tricks stakes, I was so far ahead in the joy of living stakes that Laurence, unable to catch me up on that score, would never be able to catch me up on any other score either? In fact, it was as though on the evening of her bank swindle I had exhausted my capacity for grief, as far as she was concerned, as well as any thoughts of revenge. All this, in the course of that bitter night when I had brooded over her treachery. Now it was others who were compelling me to punish her, others and doubtless myself, in anticipation of the day when pride, a sense of justice and propriety, a sense of manliness too perhaps, which was now part of my acquired character, would get the better of my inmost, passive and ultimately asocial nature. Ridiculous as it may seem, it was so as not to blame myself that I forced myself to blame Laurence.

I could not be expected to suffer greatly and to be very hurt by the actions of a person with whom I had never been – and still wasn't – madly in love; someone whose behaviour, moreover, seemed to me inspired not by any real hostility but by a kind of festering passion. Only it so happened that, for once, the most bourgeois set of people and my drop-out friends spoke with one voice, and expected me to lose my temper, to have done with the whole business. And no doubt one day I would end up thinking like them. So it was in opposition to myself that I would enter upon the last round of this fight without combatants, this trial in which some people considered me the victim and others the accused; of which, deep down, I felt myself to be only the apathetic witness. In any case, not the judge, certainly not the judge, who could not but get it wrong, whatever the role that fell to me. As for what all this was leading up to, it seemed to me that Laurence, who constantly amazed me (at last), could in all logic – her logic – just as soon attack me with a knife as share a gourmet dinner with me. In short, I was resigned to being held up to ridicule, but not for too long; I had no reserves of indignation, bitterness or resentment. Nor had I any reserves of tenderness, passion or mere feeling. And I knew that this indifference in me was quite hateful, and perhaps even hellish, to those who loved me. And it was for this reason that, in all good faith, making every allowance, I entertained two such different, possible outcomes to this crisis, both in fact worthy of a soap opera, but one melodramatic, the other bathetic. It is true that the second alternative was more in my line.

After Coriolan left, I took a long walk within Paris. I went up avenue du Maine then, beyond that, came to the old railway line that still cuts off Paris from its outskirts, throwing a belt round the city, adorned with broken bottles, nettles and bits of rail. Not a complete belt, but one that encompasses its Marshal boulevards, and constituted one of my favourite rambles. Walking along this disused track gave me the feeling of strolling through that already forgotten landscape of old westerns of the 1930s, or on the fields of battle, or on some alien and unknown planet, or of being a character involved in the fighting on the city-walls at the end of the last century, one of Carco's solitary characters, or Bradbury's, or Fitzgerald's . . . For the past week I had not even had time to read a book properly. And my bouts of depression derived as much from this as anything else.

Autumn was advancing, it was getting dark and cold earlier and earlier, and I was frozen when I pushed open the door of the Lion de Belfort at about six o'clock. Everyone was there, the *patron*, the two bystanders and Coriolan. On my arrival, the four of them looked up, returned my greeting and, as one, averted their eyes. A kind of dismay or embarrassment bore down on this place that was generally so relaxed. "Did Laurence drop by for a lemonade?" I asked Coriolan as I took a seat opposite him. But he did not even smile; he blinked, and suddenly handed me across the table the magazine he had snatched to his side on the bench when I came in. "You ought to read this," he said. I stared at him, then looked up and caught the *patron* and the two bystanders hastily focusing their attention on their drinks. What was going on here?

The magazine in question was the most widely read weekly in the whole of France, and appeared every Friday. It had surely just come out, and I was amazed that the Lion de Belfort had been in such a hurry to read it.

I opened it. I saw photos of myself filling ten pages –

blow-ups, cut-outs, full-page spreads – all of them supplied by Laurence since she was the only person who had any; photos of me as a child that had appeared from goodness knows where, one taken at my First Communion, one of me as a soldier, one at the Conservatoire with some of the other candidates, then five or six at the seaside, at home or at the door of my car, taken some time ago by Laurence, and finally, two or three snaps of the two of us sitting on a stone bench and on the terrace of a restaurant, the dullest photographs of a couple imaginable, but ones that, I knew, were ours, and the only ones we had. A slight shudder came over me. This willingness of Laurence to divulge, already considerable in terms of photographs, boded ill for the text. And sure enough, the first page began with these words: "Poets too have their madonnas." The rest, I read slowly from beginning to end. The lies and nonsense reached dizzy heights, but a jolly good story emerged: Laurence, a beautiful, rich, young lady, courted by all the most eligible bachelors of her generation, happened to go into a café on boulevard Montparnasse, where she encountered an ambitious young man with a look of torment in his eyes. She discovered that he was a composer, that he was very gifted. He fell madly in love with her at first sight, and she with him. This was a young man who could talk about music, poetry, but not about money; a young man, moreover, on the verge of destitution, an orphan. She immediately gave him everything she possessed, which was not inconsiderable. Naturally, her family was worried about his financial status, but they were swayed by his love of her, and they eventually agreed to the marriage. Only the whole affair took its toll on Laurence's mother, who died of a heart attack, and Laurence's father, unfortunately, blamed them for her death and would not have anything more to do with them. The young woman stood fast. She stood fast against an entire social circle, she stood fast against the lack of money, against an embittered father and a worried, tactless, young husband. A young husband who, to please her, was determined to succeed, who tried everything, who entered countless competitions, failing to win them, and whom she then had to console. But she was hurt by his tactlessness, especially towards her friends, for sometimes he was intent upon impressing them and let himself down, sometimes he snubbed them. She soon ended up left on her own with him, at the mercy of his whims, for he went from being most frightfully diffident to being quite insanely demanding, in order to test her feelings for him. But she loved him, oh how she loved him, she gave up everything for him, including having children – a natural enough desire in a young woman, but "When you've already one big baby, you don't have another," she told our reporter, with a charming, resigned smile. All these setbacks disheartened the young man, who became morose, and his black hair started to turn grey. One day she happened to bump into a friend of hers, a film director, and she begged him, promised him the moon if he would only give the once-ambitious young man's music a try. And the friend agreed, and for her sake defied his producers. For three months, four months, the young husband slaved away, wrote music that was too intellectual, too abstract, from which she had gently to dissuade him, very gently, lest she antagonized him and he abandoned the whole thing. One day, at last, he came up with those four notes of "Showers" and she helped him to find the rest, she sustained him "at the risk of her own sanity" and delivered him of the famous hit-song without appearing to have had anything to do with it. One evening in June – or was it July? What did the date matter? – she took this music to the hostile producer and the well-disposed film director – both of them weary, jaded, and so forth – and got them to listen to it. Depending on his original position, one of them leapt out of his chair, the other collapsed into his, but everyone bowed to the music. Success at last crowned her efforts, healing the wounded pride of her credulous husband, who delighted in the signs of this success (the ins and outs of which she did not want to reveal to him). He offered to give her everything, of course, but she refused; she wanted him to be free, to remain free to pursue his destiny, even though she herself had sacrificed her own for seven years to assure their future, their present and their past. For, whatever might fall to this young composer – even that supreme prize, that possibility of an Oscar from the United States – all the distinctions in the world would not prevent him, come evening, from seeking refuge at her side and saying to her, quaking: "Swear that you'll never leave me." Close inverted commas, end of article, end of public proclamation. I closed the magazine.

At last I understood the reason for the revival of my popularity: I had just been nominated for the Best Film Music award in Hollywood. What I did not understand was all the rest, this confused, chaotic, grotesque and putrid soap opera that Laurence was presenting as our life. It was sickening. It was worse than sickening: it was despicable, repugnant. I could understand the averted eyes of those two inane bystanders, of the *patron* of the Lion de Belfort, and even the lowered gaze of my best friend, Coriolan, sitting here opposite me.

"What can I do?" I asked.

"Nothing," said Coriolan. "You're not going to write in *La Semaine* [the other, rival weekly] that it isn't true and give your version, are you? Especially since she's twisted everything in such a way. How can you totally deny it? She uses facts . . ."

"A few distorted facts and a few half-truths," I said. "You're right, I can't deny any of it, and anyway I don't want to."

I folded my hands absent-mindedly, they did not even seem to be my own hands any more, they were the hands of a poor young husband who . . . etc. etc. I felt ashamed. For the first time in my life, I felt truly ashamed, my cheeks were on fire, and I dared not look at the other customers or the *patron*. She had even taken that away from me, the minx. Right now, I would not even dare to go shopping any more.

"And you realize what a bastard you'd appear to be if you walked out? People believe this kind of thing." Coriolan pushed the magazine back towards me with his fingernail. "And she doesn't even say a word against you. The worst that she can say, she says kindly, making it sound like softness on her part, monstrousness on yours. Ah, no, no . . ." And he shook his head, a despondent counsellor.

I found myself whistling, drumming the table with my fingertips as though I suddenly had something urgent to do, but what? Ah, yes, now I knew what it was: pack my bags. I stood up.

"Where are you going?" said Coriolan.

At my back I felt the eyes of the other three upon me. What can a young husband with feverish gaze do in such cases? I leant towards Coriolan and whispered:

"Where am I going? To pack my bags, old man."

And without waiting for a response, I left and strode off to my house, her house, the apartment in which we had cohabited after getting married.

Chapter Ten

Our faults are much keener and more assiduous than our virtues: misers are quicker to pounce on ways of saving money than the generous on opportunities to give; the proud will sooner boast than the brave belittle themselves; and the violent are fighting before the pacifists have time to intervene. The same order of priority obtains over internal dualities. My laziness had led me to adopt the mode of life offered by Laurence, long before my self-respect prompted me to find work. Laurence had entrusted me to the custody of this irresistible laziness, whilst simultaneously, in her fear of losing me, seeking another ball and chain to shackle to my feet, and she had found it: respectability. If I left her now, I was bound to appear in the eyes of the world as the ultimate bastard, as Coriolan himself had said. But Laurence was forgetting the difference in our backgrounds. She had been brought up with a respect for other people's opinion, whereas I, brought up by my semi-anarchist parents, had retained of their talk only what suited me, including a great contempt for society. Besides, my readiness to embark upon this marriage – with the all too predictable gossip that would ensue – should have informed Laurence, at any rate warned her, of this devil-may-care and provocative side to me, which would brave with relish the anger of four hundred thousand sentimental readers. Stronger than all the bounds of habit, of gratitude and of my own self-interest, as indeed of my laziness, the taste for a challenge was what drove me. Hah!

this ideal wife thought me trammelled by her stories? What a grave mistake!

I got home and began to pack my suitcase. I felt detached and relieved. This feeling that sustained me, this defiance, was neither fine nor particularly intelligent, but at least it was an irresistible feeling. (And after all, what else or what more is to be expected of our feelings if not that we should be carried away by them, without being given time to think?) I piled my clothes into a suitcase and hesitated for a moment over the acid-green suit, the first that Laurence had bought me, and which had so shamed me at the time. But I put it in with the rest. Now was no time to be choosy. I should have put my foot down straightaway, in the fitting-room, but my circumstances then had prevented me from refusing a warm suit: it would not even have occurred to me to do so. Now it was too late, and in matters of good taste, better never than too late.

I packed hastily, knowing that I would not be able to lay out and fold these future souvenirs – for all that they were made of gabardine – in Laurence's presence. From time to time, to reassure myself of being within my rights, I leant over the weekly lying open on the bed and read from it at random. "Despite all she was losing – her family, her friends, everyone in the world – the young woman never had a single regret, she knew that this man would be everything to her, as she was to him." But what did she mean by that? Could she possibly imagine that she had replaced everyone in the world, that she had "been everything" to me? I had never believed myself capable of being everything to anyone, I had never believed either that anyone could be everything to me, and besides in a certain way, I would not have wanted it. This foolish claim irritated me. I turned over the page. "They met in a café, where she saw a thin, silent young man, alone, and she fell in love with him as he fell in love with her, the moment they laid eyes upon each other."

We had indeed met in a café in Montparnasse, where I used to have a lot of fun with some great guys and a piano. She had turned up with one of her girl-friends, who was dating one of us, and had literally latched on to our group. She had gone to every length to pursue us, we really had no idea how to get rid of her. Cornelius and I had even thrown dice for dear Laurence, and it was I who won (as it were). Yes, she had fallen in love with me at first sight, but it was weeks before I could stand the sight of her and put up with her. I had gone to bed with her with some wariness, so much the archetypal bourgeois young lady did she seem to me, and her sexual passion had been a pleasant surprise . . .

I packed my shirts, books and scarves, records, camera, national lottery tickets. I left nothing but the Steinway and a few pairs of socks that I had never been able to wear because they were too warm. I closed the two cases without too much difficulty – for my trousseau was a full one but not extravagant – and without any feeling of remorse took the four pairs of cuff-links, the tie-pin and watch that constituted my spoils of war. I would also take the car. I remembered with a sense of ecstasy that the insurance had been paid and that I therefore had six months in hand. A million dollars ought to be enough to cover everything, I said to myself, with a certain pleasure in feeling small-minded.

Having packed and fastened my suitcases, I put on my famous brown, Al Capone suit and took a look at myself in the mirror. It seemed to me I looked younger already. I went over to my piano, my only regret, and for two or three minutes melancholically played a strange tune, always going back to that chord, which was becoming obsessive. As I went up and down the keyboard around those three notes, it began to pour with rain – one of those showers, appropriately enough, that made a sound of slaps and kisses. I opened the window, leant out and got some warm water on my face, and I watched and listened to it come down for a good while before closing the windows again, obligingly, thoughtfully, so as not to ruin the carpet. Then turning round, I picked up a case in each hand and went into the corridor. I would rather have said goodbye to Laurence, but I really did not have the patience to wait for her. What she would say was in any case immaterial to me, and it was with a kind of annoyance that, as I passed her bedroom, I heard her voice calling out to me.

"Vincent?"

I gave a sigh, put down my cases and went into her bedroom. It was dimly lit, as though for a night of love, and her perfume dominated it once more. I took a deep sniff of it as though to check that it was already out of date inside my head. For seven years I had spent my life enveloped by this perfume. What a strange business . . .

"Yes?"

Laurence was sitting on her bed, with her legs tucked beneath her, in a white shawl that flattered her, and she was twisting in her hands a brightly coloured silk scarf, a summer scarf.

"Sit down, please," she said. "Where were you off to?"

"I was moving out," I announced in an even voice as I sat down on the edge of the bed. "My suitcases are in the hall and I'm pleased to see you, I was worried about going without telling you."

"Moving out, moving out?"

And an immense stupefaction transformed her face. I saw her, as in novels, as in films, literally crumple before my eyes, first of all with amazement, then under the impact of an animal terror.

"Come now," I said, "you must have read that magazine, there, *L'Hebdomadaire.*"

She nodded her head, staring at me as though I were the statue of the Commendatore.

"Yes, yes," she mumbled, "yes, yes, of course I've read it. What does it matter? What is it, what does it mean, what are you talking about?"

It was my turn to be amazed. She could not possibly be unaware of the meaning of her own pathological lies, her fabrications.

"Listen, you've read it. You gave that interview, so you've read it. It's sickening, it's ignominious, it's untrue and besides, oh . . . what does it matter? I'm moving out, that's all. Our relationship has become a power struggle, in fact a hostile relationship, and I hate it.''

''But it's you! It's you that made it like that!'' She was practically shouting. ''It's you! I hate you to be like this. When I see you with that poker-face of yours, that inscrutable look, going off goodness knows where, coming back goodness knows when, and I'm forced to go out so as not to stay here waiting for you, counting the hours – you think it's I who want that? You're torturing me, Vincent! Every day you've been torturing me, every day for the past week. I haven't slept for a week, I don't know who I am any more!''

I looked at her, dumbfounded. She was obviously sincere and on the edge of a nervous breakdown. I had to get away as quickly as possible without trying to argue against her opaque and blinded view of things. I would never get anywhere, and we would hurt each other, it was pointless.

''Right.'' I stood up. ''Right, let's say it's my fault. And I'm sorry. Now, I'm going.''

''Oh, no, no!''

She had half risen from the bed, awkwardly kneeling, and she was clinging to my arm. She was about to fall, to tumble forwards, and the ludicrousness, the grotesqueness of her position would have been intolerable to me. I hastily sat down again. I did not see her any more as an ex-wife, or an enemy, or a stranger either. I saw her as a frightfully hysterical woman whom I had to get away from as quickly as possible. Her hands cautiously let go of my sleeve, as though this had been a ruse on my part. She sank back, the blood returned to her cheeks, which made me realize how pale she had been.

''Ah,'' she said, ''you frightened me . . .''

I saw with horror the tears welling from her eyes, like a shower of a different kind, as real as the one outside, before her face became distorted, her mouth twisted and she pressed her hands to her face, showing only the back of her neck to me, and her shoulders shaken with sobs.

''But where were you, what have you been doing? For the past three days, I've not lived, it's been dreadful! Oh, Vincent, the awfulness of it! But where were you? I've spent my time asking myself that question: where is he? What's he doing? What does he want? The awfulness of it! But what are we to do, Vincent? Vincent, this whole business is hateful."

I looked at her, simultaneously stupefied and detached. I reached out for her shoulders, as any gentleman acts towards a woman in tears, then at once drew back my hand. It would be cruel to touch her and to take her in my arms. She was in a bad way, she was subsisting on lies, dishonesty, preposterous lines of argument, she was blind, she must not be given further cause for aberration. She was mumbling something of which I eventually made sense:

"Where will you go? What can you do? Nothing, you can't do anything. And besides, it's rotten of you to leave me the moment you've got a bit of money to do so. Everyone's going to think you're rotten, you know that? You won't have anywhere to go, no one will help you. But what will become of you?" she asked with a genuine distress in her voice that made me want to laugh.

"All that may very well be true, but whose fault is it?"

She shrugged her shoulders as though this really was the least important question, the most trifling detail.

"It doesn't matter whose fault it is," she said, "that's the way things are. You'll die of hunger, of cold, what are you going to do?"

"I don't know," I replied firmly, "but in any case I shall not come back."

"I know," she said in a low voice, "I know very well you won't come back, that's the awful thing. For seven years I've been waiting for you to leave. For seven years I've been looking every morning to see if you're there. Every evening I look to see if you're still with me. For seven years I've been afraid of this. And now it's happened, it's happened. Ah, it can't be true! You don't realize . . ."

There was such a natural ring to her voice, to that "you don't realize", that I gazed at her with curiosity. She looked up, her eyes completely swollen, disfigured by tears as I had never seen her:

"Ah, Vincent, you can't possibly know what it is to be in love like this . . . you're lucky not to be, I assure you, you're lucky." And again she said: "You can't possibly know what it is."

When she said this to me, she spoke in a voice full of revulsion but objective in its horror, a voice that contained not the least bitterness or the least "private" grief, if I can put it that way. She was simply registering, in my presence, something that was happening to her and for which I bore virtually no responsibility. I realized this and it wrang my heart, as though she had told me she had cancer or some other fatal illness.

"But," I said, "don't you think you're exaggerating slightly? It could have been someone other than me, you know."

"Yes, but it's you, it's you. What you say doesn't make any difference, none at all, it's you. It can't be helped, and what's more, you're going away. I don't want you to go, you can't possibly be leaving, Vincent, you must understand, it's not possible: I shall die. I've fought too hard to make you stay, I've done my utmost – I've gone too far, I know – but if I'd had bars, I would have surrounded you with bars; if I'd had irons, I would have shackled you in irons; I would have walled you in to stop myself suffering like this, to be sure, sure, even for one night, one day, that you were there and that you would stay put. I would have been capable of anything."

"That's why I'm moving out," I said, vaguely scared, "it's precisely for that reason, my poor kitten," I added in spite of myself, in a final burst of pity. Because, for one moment, it was not Vincent and Laurence and that same old story of theirs that were at issue, but a man and a woman in the grip of a serious and commonplace problem called love . . . well, passion – this distinction offered me some resort.

"You don't really love me," I said. "Loving people means wishing them well, it means making them happy. You just want to keep me at your side, you said so yourself. You don't give a damn whether I'm happy, as long as I'm there."

"It's true, yes, it's true! How can I help it? You have only little troubles, little worries, inconvenience, irritation, because you aren't having enough fun or you'd like to see other people. But for me, when you turn away it's like being stabbed, you see, it's emptiness, it's heartbreak, I bang my head against walls, I tear the skin from my fingernails, I'm horrified by you, Vincent, horrified by you. You can't possibly understand."

What she said intrigued me. This was "Venus now wholly enamoured of her prey". Unfortunately, life is made of slighter sentiments – everyday life, at least.

"You must look after yourself," I said, "you must let someone calming look after you, someone who restores to you the joy of living."

She began to laugh bitterly.

"But what do you think I've been doing for seven years? I've tried doctors, psychiatrists, acupuncture, tranquillizers, physical exercise, I've done everything, tried everything, Vincent, everything. You can't possibly know what it's like." And in the only moment of altruism she ever had, she added: "It's true, it's not your fault, my poor darling, not in the least, you're even very kind on the whole, and very patient, it's true. But you're horrible too, terrible. You've never loved me, have you? Answer me! Never. You've never felt it, this heartbreak, this suffocation, this . . ." And she put her hands on her neck, over her breasts, pressing them against her body with a peculiar expression, as though she was trying to crush something between her palms and her neck. I hesitated.

"Yes, I have," I said, "I've loved you. It's something you don't understand at all, but I have loved you. I haven't lived with you for seven years without loving you, Laurence."

"You're saying that out of politeness," she cried. "Don't be polite, I beg you. Anything but that! Your politeness, your pleasant manner, your cheerfulness, your laughter, your way of breathing in the morning, of opening the window, of walking in the street, your way of drinking from a glass, of looking at women, of looking at me, even me, your appetite for life – it's horrible, it kills me! You'll never be able to escape that, no more that I can escape you. It's hopeless, hopeless!"

"Yes," I said, with a feeling of happiness, "yes, it's hopeless."

She reached her hand out towards me, cautiously touched my shoulder.

"So you see," she went on, "given that it's hopeless, you're not going to tell me, as well, that you are going? That's too much. It's beyond endurance. You can't be leaving, Vincent?"

I confess, I was speechless. Little by little, a sense of her wretchedness, of her unhappiness, of the enormity of that unhappiness, which I perceived with a degree of fear, awakened in me a kind of sad shame, a great desire to try to do something for this human being writhing before me on this bed; with the texture of whose skin, with whose breath, whose way of making love, whose voice, whose sleep, I was familiar, and of whom I knew nothing else. I had never had any understanding of Laurence at all. I had said to myself that she loved me a little too much, without imagining that this "little too much" might be costing her a life of hell. And it was all very well actually knowing her to be stupid, despicable, spiteful, selfish and blind, I could not help vaguely admiring her for that something that I did not know, that I would probably never know, that I did not wish to know, even while slightly regretting it. Was this what it was to be madly in love? No, this was wretched passion, something completely different. In love, I knew, there was laughter. We had never laughed together, never really laughed.

"Listen," I said, "there's no point in my staying. I've tried, for your sake, for me, for us, but it can't last. I can't bear this dependence on you any more, the exhibitionism of our lives, these magazines, this dross around us – I really can't."

She had heard only a single word: dependence. And she pounced upon her bedside table with a peculiar cry, grabbed her handbag, pulled out a chequebook and to my great astonishment began to scribble on it.

"Whatever you want," she cried, "whatever you want, I'll give it back to you right now, here, look, a cheque, two cheques, three cheques, it's our joint-account chequebook, I went to get it this afternoon. Look, I'm signing them all, you can take all your money tomorrow, the day after tomorrow, mine as well, if you want. Take it all back, do what you like, spend it, blow it, give it to your friends, do what you like but don't leave, I beg you, Vincent, don't leave. Listen, even if I give you one cheque, just one, you can take everything back with it, you know? Will you stay?"

I had stood up and was staring at her with disgust. This tearful woman, signing a half-torn chequebook with a pen, and with hands already stained with ink, put me to shame. Like some defeated gaoler, she was undoing what she had taken so long to arrange – my capture. And I was angry with myself for not being able to take advantage of this defeat; I did not have the heart for it right now. It was foolish, but I could not take any of those cheques, just one of which would have been enough.

"Take it, I beg of you," she said in a low voice, staring at me, unmoving. "Take it, please. Stay and take it, but don't leave. Three days, two days, stay three days, two days if you like, but don't leave this evening. I beg of you, Vincent."

She held one of those famous cheques, signed in her name, right in front of me. I wavered. If I took it, at all events I would have to stay a while; and maybe my cynicism would resurface and compel me to clear out some other day. But I could not take it if I was sure of leaving. After all, it was my money, why shouldn't I take it? Yes, but she would interpret it as a promise, and it would be horrible to lie to her now. On the other hand, if I didn't take it, I was in a fix. I would sink into poverty with Coriolan, and no one could tell how it would end. Of course, it was my money, but it did not belong to me any more, insofar as she was giving it back to me. These thoughts tumbled and jostled inside my head. My sense of morality – or at least, the little I had of any – vied with my strongest instincts. The dual feeling of horror and pity that Laurence inspired in me did not help. I was decidedly unaccustomed to these moral clashes between me and myself.

So it was that I suddenly found it simpler to follow my two strongest and least conflicting impulses. I took the chequebook and stuffed it into my pocket in order to save myself from poverty, then I took Laurence in my arms and held her close to me to save her from distress. Other than these two gestures, I really did not see what else I could do that was natural and decent, or, as they say, human.

"Oh, Vincent," mumbled Laurence, pressed against me, "forgive me, I shan't ever do that to you again, I've been selfish, hateful, I hurt you, I humiliated you, I tried everything, I didn't know how else to wipe that genial and trusting smile off your face, that look of being elsewhere. I shall never do it again, I promise you, never again. I'll try to make you happy."

"That's more than I ask of you," I said, patting her head, "that's more than I ask of you. Just try to be a little happy and not to treat me like a lap dog. Be kind and gentle again, you must become gentle again, you were so much better like that."

She was half suffocating, she was giving hoarse little cries, whether of relief, sorrow, or fear too close at hand, I did not know.

"I swear to you," she said, "I swear to you. I must explain to you why I was like that. It's panic, you see . . ."

She embarked on a long and terrible story, a horror film, in which she did not spare herself (me neither, actually) and from which it emerged that Racine had not exaggerated, nor had any of those novels that I had read with so much respect and surprise. Laurence spoke to me of feelings just as unbearable, just as extreme. I could not see how she came by such passion, there was not within her anybody cut out for it. It was as though a poetic genius had been thrust upon my father-in-law.

But the more she talked, the more I realized that for seven years I had been the helpless witness to feelings I had done nothing to arouse, at the same time being culpably heedless of them. Yes, I was guilty, guilty of not having seen anything – if not of actually having done anything to her. I told myself with virtuous tenderness that I was going to help her, that I would take her everywhere with me, even to the races, that I would patch things up between her and Coriolan, and that little by little I would teach her to laugh at her own excesses, to cool the flames of her passion with irony before getting burned. "Poor Laurence, poor child, poor grown-up little girl," I said to myself, as I rocked her.

And later on in the evening, in the intimacy of that dark, dark bedroom, while she dwelt upon that tale – a tale of such extremity and so unrelieved, too – it was pity, it was compassion that allowed me to prove to Laurence my love for her, in the only way of which I was capable. And sure enough, these motions reassured her.

As for myself, I felt shocked by the drive and indifference of my own body.

Chapter Eleven

I awoke with my head on Laurence's arm. I immediately rediscovered the smell and texture of her skin, her perfume and a feeling, as it were, of contentment and peace, increased tenfold by the memory of those crumpled but signed cheques in the pocket of my trousers on the floor. This woman's mental stability, Coriolan's survival, my own independence lay there quietly on the carpet, at my feet.

Poor Laurence! She too lay quiet, far, far removed, it seemed, from the thorns and prickles of her passion. I would do all I could from now on, I said to myself, to contain or alleviate this devilish obsession. I personally would have so hated to suffer anything of that kind, I would have so hated to be in her place. Meanwhile, I examined my wife's features. She had imagination's broad brow, the high cheek-bones of pride, and the mouth – determined above and sensual below – that symbolizes the duality of so many modern women. If only she resigned herself to not confusing her own little ways with moral laws, and her whims with duties, life would be much easier for her. In the meantime, she was not to renew her tyrannies in the name of her passion. I had been sufficiently trounced morally, sufficiently disheartened by her scheming! Nor was the thought of the ridicule and sarcastic remarks that still awaited me in the outside world a particularly pleasant one. No, together, here and now, we should take certain measures and even certain "decisions that there would be no going back on".

Carried away by these noble plans, I tore myself out of bed and with a firm step went to open the shutters of her bedroom that had again become "our" bedroom, to take a deep breath of fresh air. I left the window on the catch, half-open, but dutifully mindful of Laurence's mother, I came back to pull the blankets over her shoulders. She opened her eyes, blinked, saw me, and offered her mouth to me, rounded for a kiss. (Some importunate person inside me let out an ugly oath.) I planted a quick kiss on her lips and went off to my studio. There, I threw myself on that war-bed I thought I had left behind me twelve hours earlier, and stretched out on it, happy to be alone again. I had in a very short space of time acquired several habits that I would have difficulty in breaking so quickly. It must be said that it was barely a week since I had been to see Not-a-sou demanding money from him. The time had passed like lightning, lightning that had ravaged trees and minds, shaken horse-chestnuts and hearts. (From time to time, that talkative little voice inside me made itself heard again, more or less wittingly.)

It was nevertheless miraculous that all these ups and downs had left me none the worse for wear, in fine fettle, in good humour; moreover, a kind of amusement, a cynical mirth that I might describe as post-operative caused a tingling in my legs, in my head, and prevented me from sleeping. I got up again, went to my handsome piano – when all was said and done, the most concrete, most serious trace of that unreal week – and unthinkingly struck my famous chord. Twelve notes followed it at once without my paying attention, once, twice, three times, until I tried to attribute an origin to them, a voice, a context. In vain, I played that melodic line as rock, as pop, as jazz, in slow time, as a waltz, I searched for words in French, English, Spanish, I searched for a film . . . goodness knows, it rejected every singer's name, every orchestra, every suggestion my memory volunteered. Nothing. Then I played those notes once more, as I heard them, I set them off again and listened to them answering each other, every one in its place and every one indispensable, all of them fluid. And I let others, just as obvious, develop after them, until they had formed a complete tune, a melody, a song, whatever, but something that I wrote down at once in my music notebook: something that was musically attractive, that was catchy and tender, light-hearted and sad at the same time, music that was virtually irresistible.

And I would kill anyone who dared to deny that this music was mine, that it belonged to me, to no one else but me, and to me alone. It was "my" music. I could now take those cheques in my pocket and throw them out of the window, they were of no importance any more. All that quarrelling had been a sombre but instructive joke made dramatic by the inexistence of these twelve notes too belatedly come into being. Unless they were born of this bitter affair? Or of . . . I was not sure of anything any more, except that they were there, that I was playing them again and again, tirelessly, louder and louder, loud enough to waken the whole building. But the building did not stir. Fortunately, for I was exultant. And, with me, exultation was very close to a happy frenzy that brooked no interruption.

The whole of my tune followed from that chord, that famous and singular chord that I had been playing non-stop, and without realizing it, for four days now, that chord about which Coriolan had asked me where it came from, without insisting, and without my giving him an answer, of course. How could I have thought that those three notes would lead to a development of this kind, would bring forth the twelve or fourteen sister-notes that followed of themselves? This spirited and tender music would lend itself to the interrupted cadences and tempos of modern rhythms as well as to the languor of a solitary piano. I sketched out the skeleton of it, I picked out the notes of this leitmotiv one by one or in continuous sequence, fifty times, marvelling each time at their complicity. I would repeat the introduction twice, in bass, then I would take it away with a clarinet, a saxophone, a piano and a guitar, and finally the voice would come in, a deep, physical voice, a husky voice – this song needed a voice both husky and universal. It was music that evoked regrets, but happy regrets. I did not really know how a musical success came about, but I knew that, upon hearing it again later, people would remember having loved someone to this tune, danced to this tune, been blessed by heaven to this tune. This was what it expressed, but could you call a piece of music "Happy Regrets"? Who cared? The main thing about a piece of music was that the memory of it should stir your feelings, and so it would be with this music. I was mad with joy, not proud of myself but on the contrary modest for once, too. In a moment of possessive panic, I wrote it down ten or twelve times on different sheets of music paper, which I hid in the four corners of my studio.

Then, as a final test, I telephoned Coriolan and played him my new-born piece on the piano over the telephone. I immediately heard his silence, so to speak. And afterwards I heard him tell me it was an entirely new piece of music, he was sure of it, it was superb, there was something exhilarating in it, it did not exist before now, he would swear to it, and he bet me a bottle of whisky, or ten bottles, it would be the greatest success of the century, etc. etc. All this, I lapped up, for I knew that Coriolan was capable of lying about anything except music. I felt I was a composer at last, and for the first time – for "Showers" had come into being in the corner of a studio and had been rehearsed and played only two hours before being scored and slipped, like a thief, into the film, in the bits where it flagged. But this tune, these "Happy Regrets", no, they would have trouble taking it away from me and turning it into anything other than music for meeting, being attracted to each other, loving each other, then cherishing or missing each other. And, paranoid, as the worst amateur painter becomes paranoid upon completing his work, I did not want my music merely to evoke all these feelings; paranoid then, I wanted it to compel them.

So when I realized that the motionless patch of white on the threshold of my studio, at the extreme periphery of my vision, was Laurence, and also that she had been standing there for a good ten minutes, I was torn between fear that she had seen my look of idiotic bliss, and delight that she should have been so transfixed by the charm of my music.

I swivelled round on my chair and gazed at her. Wearing a gossamer negligée over her transparent nightdress, looking very pale with those big eyes, she was quite a romantic sight.

"What do you think of it?" I asked, smiling.

Turning back to my piano, I played my music again to a slow samba rhythm, a South American rhythm such as I knew she liked.

"Who's it by?" I heard from behind me, and without even turning round I said:

"Guess! It's your favourite musician, my darling."

The silence that followed did not hit me until six or seven seconds afterwards, and I turned round. I saw her face harden and I knew that it was all over even before she came towards me, like a pythoness, hissing horrors between her teeth.

"You knew yesterday, didn't you? You found the courage to leave because you knew that you had some money coming to you, that you were going to earn some? You were leaving because you didn't need me any more, did you? But when you saw that cheque on our joint account, you actually hesitated, you said to yourself: What a pity! I wondered what was making you so courageous, I couldn't work it out!"

I in turn rose to my feet, I stood in front of my piano and stared at her, speechless. Simply speechless, with no other reaction. This must have made her even more furious, for she came up to my piano and started beating it with her fists and scratching it with her fingernails.

"You thought yourself clever, did you? Well, I'm going to tell you something: it'll be just as well for you if that blessed music is successful! Because that cheque, that famous cheque I gave you yesterday – well, I'm going to stop it, my poor friend! On a joint account, believe me, stopping a cheque is taken seriously. You said to yourself that one night for a million dollars was perhaps worth it? You thought yourself clever? And you took me for a fool, a fool, a fool?"

She yelled louder and louder: "A fool, a fool?" She yelled, she was half-naked, and beside herself; she was turning ugly. It was so as not to have to look at her any more that I ran out into the corridor. I was no longer running away from dishonesty, or stupidity, or harshness, or anything abstract, I was running away from a madwoman who did not love me and who was shouting too loudly. I picked up my bags in the hall, threw them into the car and drove off. Ten minutes later I passed through Porte d'Orléans.

The countryside was beautiful, green, a genuine Pissarro, and with all the windows open, I breathed in through my car-door window the damp-earth smell you get in the month of October. I must have had five thousand francs on me; I would try to make them last and to spend as long as possible on the road. When I had no money left, I would go back to see Coriolan. Meanwhile, I needed some air.

At about ten in the morning the sun came out from behind the clouds and I thought that if my new music was a success, if I became rich again, I would buy myself a convertible. At eleven I was on the outskirts of Sens and the jazz concert I had been listening to until then ended. I wanted to whistle my famous tune, but I could not remember it. After a moment's searching for it in vain, I rang Coriolan who was out. Finally, I remembered the ten copies I had hidden in the studio, and decided to call Odile, who had some knowledge of music, so that she could hum it to me quietly over the phone.

It took her a long time to pick up the receiver and it took me a long time to make out through her sobs that Laurence had thrown herself out of the window after my departure, and that she was dead. She had taken the trouble to put on a more respectable nightgown before jumping.

The cars were travelling very fast on the motorway. I did a U-turn as soon as I could and headed back for Paris. Half-way there, my music came back to me. I whistled it, stubbornly, between my teeth, all the way to boulevard Raspail.